UPTOWN QUICKSAND

R.T. GRAVES

For Lilly

CONTENTS

PROLOGUE

Some people are natural born storytellers. Put them in a room with anyone and their mouths will open, for better or worse. Then there are those more reserved or sullen folks who will not, often cannot, and, more often than not, should not tell a story. I have been described as a loquacious man (I recall my first ex-wife using the words "garrulous bastard"), but that doesn't mean I tell many stories. In fact I have a very small circulation of stories because at the ripe age of forty-seven I barely remember any stories worth telling. Besides, most people don't want to hear the stories I remember for one reason or another.

So it's a good thing that I don't write for people. I don't like people. Many don't like me. I like horses and hounds. Most of them don't like me either. In truth, I write for my unborn daughter. She deserves the story. If the day comes where she asks how the hell I ended up with such atrocious debts to Manhattan's best criminal and civil attorneys, I can hand her this story.

Now, it strikes me as appropriate to start again by stating something plain: Nothing is as it seems. Not at the beginning when you're looking to do the right thing and win over a girl. Not in the middle when you're getting

1

pistol-whipped (literally or figuratively). Not at the end when you're being carted down a hallway on your back with gun shot wounds, bleeding like only an unlucky idiot can. Not ever.

Take shit for granted. I'll wager heavily that it comes back to bite you in the ass (assuming you're giving decent odds) because I've made that mistake. My ass is littered with bite marks from years of colossal oversights. And my big mistakes trump forgetting to floss or getting an adjustable rate mortgage. My mistakes are blinding, bullet-attractions. Tragically and regularly, I forget my creed that "Nothing is as it seems".

Also, it doesn't help that I've spent the better part of my life and my entire career chasing degenerates. This is useful information as the stories I do end up telling are always about how I got involved with the wrong people, how I pissed them off and how they tried to bury me.

There's a saying: "He that seeks trouble never misses". I like that. It makes sense. I don't seek trouble. Trouble just seems to know where I am. At all times. I hate that. I mind even a moderate amount of trouble. But I've learned to accept it as a part of life. I've learned trouble is quicksand. Sooner or later you run into it. When you do, you don't know you have. And the harder you struggle; the quicker you try to get out, the easier you sink. Much to my chagrin, quicksand and I have got a special thing going.

CHAPTER ONE

The P.I. game isn't what it used to be. It never was like what you see in the movies or read in the books. There was never any glitz or glamour. And in all my years, I never met a hero doing this job. Shitty pay, sporadic employment, sleazy tactics and the inability to get away with crimes that cops do, doesn't attract heroes. It attracts the desperate, tarnished and callous. I didn't always meet the criteria for a P.I. I was a cop once. I was no super cop- no Frank Serpico, no John McClane, but I made my collars, and I did most of what I was asked. As a private detective, I'm no Sam Spade, no Jake Gittes. I do my job and I go home. Generally, I like to do my job just well enough to stay above ground.

August is a terrible fucking month, and New York gets savage. People leave town. I can't blame them. I would, if I could. Worse, though, is the heat. I hate the heat. Nothing feels right. There's nothing lovable about the combination of all the lawyers leaving town so there's no business, and the sun being five inches from my fucking face.

No private investigator gets much business in late August. Like I said, people leave town. People forget about screwing around, finding their biological parents or doing a

3

background check on their sinister looking neighbor. Lawyers flee for the safety of Sag Harbor or Martha's Vineyard or wherever the bloodsuckers congregate. Just the same, I love my lawyers, my bastard children and my philanderers. I make my bread and butter off lawyers and philanderers. Lawyers hire me as a handy man. I fix the little things and take care of all the small shit they need done before depositions, arbitrations, trials, whatever. Jealous wives and egomaniacal husbands hand me the rest of my dough.

A husband and wife both hired me separately once, each to keep tabs on the other. They were both cheating. They both got proof. They got their money's worth. I considered scheduling them with the same appointment time, just to watch sparks fly. In the end, I figured I'd rather collect my checks and keep everything in my office in one piece.

So that's how I spend most of my days, doing whatever I must and avoiding debacles.

But the particular job I hereby intend to detail was not my standard fare. No insidious legal eagle, unkempt husband or wary wife engaged my services. This beastly, bitch of a case was hand delivered to my office. It came in a pretty little package with blonde hair and a sharp jaw, but she should've had "Devious wench, handle with care" tattooed on her forehead.

I was up by nine, jabbing at my alarm clock. The manila folder hovered on my bedside table. "Graves" was written across the front in Hal's chicken scratch. I thumbed through the photos again, half awake. Hal had scribbled, "Ten AM." on a post-it note. So I showered, brushed my teeth and hair, tied my shoes real tight and was off. On my way out the door my good start took a shit turn.

Ralph Sharpe sat on the stairs between my floor and the next landing. Sharpe was a walking public service announcement for the dangers of everything unhealthy.

He was smelly, greasy, and resembled a drumstick. Along with being a general hazard, he was a collector. Sal had been my bookie since I had let him give me the slip when I worked anti-crime in the early 80's. A twenty-year relationship is a long relationship, sadly. It was about the longest relationship I could claim. But I wasn't a cop anymore and I hadn't been for years, so he wasn't letting me give him the slip. I had picked some losers at the track and a few more on the diamond. I owed. I owed a pretty large chunk of change in fact, and that is why Ralph Sharpe was sitting on the stairs between my floor and the next landing.

"How ya doing, Graves?"

"Who let you out of your cage?"

"The number's piling up. The vig ain't getting any smaller as time goes by."

"Who do I call in this situation? The zoo or animal control?"

"Sal says you have until the end of the week. You guys go back a long time but--"

"I'm pretty familiar with how the placing bets and paying debts shit works, Ralph."

"Good 'cause you ain't a cop no more. You got nothing to offer. So you pay like everyone else."

"Yeah. Like your wife always says,"

Now Sharpe stood in the doorway. I'd managed to herd Ralph down to the vestibule. He threw me against the wall with the mailboxes. I craned my neck in a futile effort to avoid his breath.

"The money by the end of the week, motherfucker."

Sharpe exited. I gathered myself, made sure my suit coat was neatly resting over my forearm and cracked my neck.

My neck had been feeling good, but it started to act up then. I have a bad neck and back. I got into a jam when I was younger, the most tolerable repercussions of which were the agonizing damages to my cervical and thoracic vertebrae. Doctors with God complexes and holistic alternatives have all taken their shots. Inevitably, they all tell me the same thing, "There ain't no fixing you. So keep your weight down, limit the strains and try not to crack your neck." The neck cracking is one of those habits that I'm either unwilling or unable to give up. Like snacking, drinking, gambling and marrying women.

I stepped out on to the sidewalk, moaning as I felt the heat. I walked slowly. I was on my way to being drenched in sweat as I walked into the coffee shop across from the Marriot around 49 and Lex. I walked out blowing on the coffee. A woman walked out behind me with an iced coffee. I held the door for her. She had a kid in a stroller.

"Now, that was a good idea." I pointed at her coffee. "The iced coffee. Not the kid."

She smiled and nodded. I made a face at the kid. As they strolled away, I saw him. Then I spotted her. They walked into the hotel. I dumped the coffee and crossed the street to get a better look. I acted inconspicuous, though part of me wanted him to recognize me right then. I had to lean into the bellboy to see them check in. He didn't seem too comfortable with how close I was.

"Can I help you with something, sir?"

"Nope"

I had my eyes fixed on the sniveling little maggot. I couldn't see the appeal.

"Sniveling cocksucker" The bellboy gave me an incredulous stare. "Don't mind me, kid. I'm just a jealous dick. Lose the coat. It's hot. Far too fucking hot."

"Yeah… You too"

I stomped off. I was pissed. I was feeling self-righteous. And I didn't know what to do about what I had just seen. I was sweating my balls off walking to the office. I didn't even get there until 10:30. Sadly, it wasn't that astonishing. It must have been a Wednesday. But it could have been a Thursday. Shit, it was probably Monday. Renee was behind her desk. Her right arm was securely planted on the desk, propping up her head.

I remember Renee being particularly pissy that morning. I remember that vividly. She started up with me immediately.

"Graves, I swear to god if you don't get a better air conditioner I am going to burst into flames and bring this whole office down with me."

"I'll check with management."

"Not funny, Graves. It's August."

"Exactly. Summer's almost over. You've just got to grind it out a bit longer. I know you will. You're so damn tough."

"Fuck you very much."

"Why aren't you sitting in my office with the good air conditioner?"

"I would, but unfortunately you have some business."

"Someone's waiting?"

"Yes, your new client, a walk in. I felt for the good of the business I shouldn't allow her to boil out here."

"Good thinking. Who is she?"

"Walk through the door and solve the mystery yourself, super dick."

"You're so cute in the mornings."

She gave me the finger before reverting to her previous position on the desk. I opened the door in to my office. The first thing I saw was her hair. Bright and blonde. She was jumpy. She flipped around to make sure it was me. Then she moved her head back and stared straight at my desk. I walked around her and sat down.

"Hello."

"Is this how you run your business? It's 10:45. Do you arrive at 10:45 everyday?"

"My apologies, but I don't remember having an appointment this morning."

"I can't make an appointment if no one's here."

"Sure you can. We have an answering machine. The number is etched right there on the glass. All you need is a quarter and a voice."

"I guess I should go make an appointment then."

"No... I'm sorry. Don't bother. You're here now, right?"

"I guess."

"How can I help you...I didn't catch your name..."

"Why does that matter?"

"A name would be a good place to start."

"...Heather Lawson."

"Alright, Ms. Lawson? Mrs. Lawson?"

"Ms. Lawson"

"Ms. Lawson, what can I do for you?"

"You are Graves, right? You used to be a cop."

"Not the one and only, but yeah--"

"You used to be a cop?"

"Something like that. I'm not employed by the NYPD anymore. If that's what you wanted--"

"Okay. What does RT stand for?"

"That's private. People call me Graves. You can call me whatever makes you content when it comes time to sign the checks."

"Okay. Mr. Graves, I need you to find somebody. Well... Yes, I need you to find someone for me."

"Who's that?"

"Michael Lawson"

"Husband?"

"No. Why would you think that?"

"Same last name"

"He's my brother"

"How long has it been since you've seen him?"

"Over six years."

"And where was he the last time you saw him?"

"I had a drink with him. It must've been—It'll be 7 years ago at Christmas. We met for a drink."

"Where?"

"The Carlyle"

"Was he staying there?"

"No, he wasn't staying there."

"Well, if you want me to run him down, I am going to need you to sign a contract and leave a deposit as a retainer. Then I'm going to need whatever you can tell me about him. Age, height, weight, eye color, spouses, significant others, occupation, hobbies, phone numbers, residences would all be helpful in tracking down your brother."

I couldn't find a pad on my desk. I pulled out the top two drawers on my left without spotting a notepad. I noticed that I had left the key to the bottom drawer in the lock of the bottom drawer. I turned it. I opened the drawer; saw my gun, holster, extra clips and bullets. I threw the manila folder from my jacket into the drawer. I closed it back up, turned the key and threw it in my pocket. I finally found a pad in one of the drawers on the right. The top few pages were doodles and bullshit so I ripped them off. I found a pen and clicked it down.

"Michael's about six feet tall, he's got-- Here just take this." She had a piece of notebook paper with notes of his description scribbled all over it. It read: brown hair, brown eyes, 6 ft, left handed, birthday is 11-15-73, sculptor, artist, tennis, sober since '99, Buddhist.

"Okay. Good"

"I wrote it on the subway on the way up here. I tried to think of everything that could be helpful."

"This is good. Sculptor?"

"Abstract, minimalist. He could make something beautiful out of anything. He's gifted like that. It was his calling."

"Must be nice, having a calling."

"He majored in art history in college, but he just wanted to make art."

"What college?"

"Brown. ...Our father made sure he was an art history major. So much more reputable than an art major. When Michael graduated, he made Michael work for him.

Michael was devastated. He hated it. The whole thing set him back for a long time."

"Sure. What did…does your father do?"

"He's--He's in shipping."

"Shipping? As in boats or--Leo Lawson's Lawson?"

"You know him?"

"No. Not personally."

"Than how do you know about his--"

"When you have as much money as your father, you get a fan club. Even private detectives aren't immune to envy."

"Believe me, there is nothing to envy in that man."

"All right. But I have to ask Ms. Lawson: Why isn't your father concerned about your brother's disappearance?"

"They had a falling out. They don't speak."

"Are you certain?"

"Yes"

"But why isn't he concerned?"

"Look, Mr. Graves. I don't want to talk about Leo Lawson or why he is or isn't concerned. I honestly don't know. All I want to do is find Michael. Can you, or can't you, help me with that?"

"I can. Was he born here?"

"In the city? Yes."

"Missing six years?"

"Almost seven"

"So Ms. Lawson, why now after seven years? What are you really looking for?"

"To find--"

"A missing persons case is usually something for the police."

"No. No, he's not missing. I just don't know where he is. If that makes any sense--"

"Okay. Well, you're looking for your brother who has been gone for almost seven years. That either means that one of you did not want to see the other or one of you was somewhere where one couldn't reach the other. So either he's going to be hard to find or he doesn't want to be found. Why did Michael want to disappear?"

"I'll pay you whatever your salary is."

"That's not my concern here."

"Mr. Graves, I love Michael. I am worried and I have wanted to see him for many years. I've been to other private detectives. They either turned down the case or came up with nothing. I was referred to you. Will you take the case or not?"

"I'll take the case. But there's a good chance it's a fool's errand. He's been gone a long time, so I don't guarantee anything. You'll be charged a retainer, an hourly rate, and all expenses are paid, whether or not I find Michael. If I hit a dead end, I won't waste my time, or your money. That's it. Case closed."

"Fine"

"My secretary will draw up the contract. You can sign it, and leave a check on your way out."

I hit the intercom button on the phone and asked Renee to draw up a standard missing person contract for Ms. Lawson. Renee knew that meant she had to hike up the retainer and my rate too. What can I say? I suffer perpetual recessions.

"If there's nothing else Ms. Lawson, I won't take up anymore of your time. I'll get right to work."

"How will you keep me posted on your progress?"

"There's a place on the contract to write down all your contact information. I'll call you."

"I'm not sure where I'll be."

"Cell phone number?"

"Yeah, I guess I could give you that."

"That should be enough. You know where I work too. One way or another you should be able to get me."

"Do you have a card?"

"Help yourself."

Heather's hands were small and pale. The nail polish on

her nails was so worn it was barely visible. She struggled with the stack of cards on my desk. It took her a few moments to single out one business card and remove it from the stack.

"How will you track him down?"

"I have my ways. These days it's very hard to live off the grid. At one point or another, your name goes into a computer somewhere. One system or agency will have some information on his whereabouts. It's all about who you know and finding out what you can. And then connecting the little dots so you can see the big picture. We've just got to hope he's not living with jungle people in the Amazon. My connections are limited there."

"Okay. Just one thing, Mr. Graves."

"I'm your servant, Ms. Lawson."

"Don't contact my father about this. I don't want him to know anything about it. I don't want anyone to know anything about this except for you and me."

"All right"

"Thank you, Mr. Graves."

"My pleasure, Ms. Lawson"

She was petit, thin and jittery as she walked towards Renee. Leaning in the doorway to my office, I watched her apprehensively write some information on the contract, sign and retrieve her copy. Renee asked for a check. Heather pulled out a wad of cash. Renee counted it off with one eyebrow raised. Heather nodded, twitched and slammed the outer office door behind her. Renee was immediately off put.

"She was weird."

"Weird?"

"Yes, Graves. Weird. Do you need me to get the dictionary out?"

"She's strung out."

"Like drugs?"

"Like drugs."

"You got to know her that well, huh?"

"A girl doesn't let herself start looking like that without Charlie's help."

"Charlie?"

"Cocaine. Need a dictionary?"

"You know you're not really witty. Just annoying."

"You just think that because I'm the boss of you. Now, what incredibly important task are—ah—Solitaire."

She was playing solitaire on her computer. I cracked my neck. I hovered over her shoulder. I could almost see the cards without my glasses.

"Red seven on black eight"

"Where?"

"There"

"That's a six."

"Oh. Is there any coffee left?"

"I don't drink your coffee."

"You know that most secretaries attempt to aid their employers in their daily... enterprises and endeavors...or at least they pretend to."

"I'm not most secretaries."

"You certainly are not."

"I'm your secretary. And your secretary doesn't make you coffee. She does your books, deposits your checks, organizes your appointments and generally runs your life."

"Right. It's a good thing you're here to tell me these things."

"What's the job for our young strung out blonde?"

"Finding Michael Lawson. Brother, sculptor, Buddhist."

"Maybe he makes begging bowls."

"Abstract statues and shit"

"I think I'd rather have a bowl."

"Maybe he'll make me a coffee mug after I reunite him with his sister."

I spent the afternoon running down the usual avenues on the computer, and over the phone. I ended up calling Pierce. Pierce Champlain was my old partner. We worked anti-crime together when we were young. Then we got partnered up again after we made detective. We were partners for 16 years. That was a rarity in our day. Not many made it that long. He was my best friend by default. Once I became a private dick I was just too lazy to get a new one.

"Hey"

"What do you want?"

"What crawled up your ass?"

"A gentle Uzbekistani from Little Odessa just bashed in the knee caps of one of my C.I.'s."

"That should prove to be amusing."

"What do you want, Graves? I seriously do not have the time for this."

"Don't get your panties in a bundle. I want you to run someone for me."

"No. I'm not running anyone for you."

He hung up. I called him back.

"Why are you hanging up on me? I'm not your wife."

"Graves, I do not have the time to fuck around doing your job."

"Come on, sweetheart. It's easier if you do it. Do a partner a favor?"

"You're not my partner. My partner is a vigilant slender justice junkie. You're more like a fat leach attached to my balls."

His partner, Billy Caruso, was well over three hundred pounds, never without a stained tie and his barber had to be a fucking chimpanzee. Since making sergeant in his twenties, Billy had been acting like a beleaguered veteran. Unfortunately for Pierce, Billy was a staple in the Organized Crime Unit and his wife was the Deputy of Operations' favorite niece. I thought I heard him snoring in the background but that very well could have just been his normal breathing.

"Leach. That is harsh, my friend."

"I really don't have time, Graves. I'll talk--"

"Michael Lionel Lawson. D.O.B.: 11-15-73. He's a native, son of the shipping tycoon. Just jot it down. Run him through if you get a second, which I think you will."

"Lawson, Michael Lionel. 11-15-73 Goodbye"

I worked on the kid all afternoon. It was a ghostly existence for young Mr. Lawson. Michael Lionel Lawson never had a driver's license. He never had a mortgage or paid a utility bill. He enrolled as a member of Brown's class of 1994, but he never graduated. He was an art history major with an Asian Studies minor. Heather had been right about that. She had also been right about him working for his father. He only declared an income three times, from '93 to '96. He listed his employer as Lawson Shipping, Inc. By '98 he had credit card statements being delivered to a loft in SoHo rented by Leo Lawson.

Everything ran through Leo. He popped up everywhere. I assumed he flipped all Michael's bills. Leo inherited a small shipping company at twenty-seven with the death of his father. From there, Leo built his own little empire, complete with a stiff upper lip, tight asshole, and more riches than any many should know. He had just turned 71.

I gathered some additional bullshit here and there, but nothing that didn't definitively lead to Leo Lawson. Once Pierce called me back to tell me the guy had no criminal record, I was desperate to milk a few more hours work out of the job. I was drooling over the idea of even a measly bonus at the end of the rainbow. A thought which seems nothing short of comical given what I know now.

CHAPTER TWO

I didn't have a good picture of the kid, both literally and figuratively. Since my calls had gone dead and I needed to make some headway, I did the most irregular of things. I took some initiative. It was nearing the end of the workday, about 4 o'clock, and Renee was on the phone with a girlfriend.

"Close up for me?"

"A bit early to be heading out isn't it? Can't you even make to 4?"

"You see any appointments on the horizon? And for your edification, I'm actually on the job right now, babe. I'm going to go see a man about some dirt."

"Who?"

"He's the son of a very rich man, very upper crust, very suave, very social. They're a well-known and respectable family in many circles. Small circles though, you wouldn't fit."

"Very funny. You can fuck off, now."

Renee was too good to and for me. She hadn't sued me for sexual harassment, was jovial, intelligent and had a sense of humor. For the last two years she'd been the only real staple in my life. To boot, she was a true brunette with legs, style and sass. Unfortunately she had made the mistake of marrying a greasy advertising executive who drank, played and partied too much. She was near perfect. Her husband and I tussled; often verbally and once physically. He ended up breaking his hand. I hated that prick. The shithead broke it himself, but I ended up on the ropes with Renee for a few weeks. I thought she would've quit. But she stuck around for one reason or another. It was probably because she pitied me. I didn't care. She was still around. I could take her for granted and that's what I liked. She was someone to rely on and admire from a distance.

I put my suit coat over my arm, and rolled up my sleeves as I headed uptown. It was cooling down, but still hot. I got to the entrance to the subway station, turned and splurged on a cab. It wasn't that far uptown, but it was far enough not to look forward to the subway.

Riding in the cab up Central Park West, I prayed that he would let me in. I didn't want to call him because it would be too easy for him to schedule me for an appointment next year. When I need to find an ex-cop I go see a friend in records at Police Plaza. When I need to find a deadbeat druggie, I go looking for some talkative pushers in their part of town. When I need to find some yuppie, sculpting, Ivy League drop out and his dirty laundry, I go looking for Samuel Garcia. That's just how it is.

Garcia was rich. He didn't claw his way to the top of the corporate ladder, make shady business deals or artfully scam anyone out of their money. Sam got his money gracefully, inheriting a small fortune. His father was rich and Spanish. His mother was Latvian and either a dancer or a dentist. I can't remember which but either was an odd fit for the son of a Spanish industrialist. He grew up somewhere. Not sure where, but he grew up. Then he traveled. He was one of those worldly stiffs. He knew a shit load about shit but couldn't spot shit if it was flung at him. Just the same, Samuel Garcia was a good enough apple. He had his faults, but snobbery wasn't one of them. He'd never inspire you to puke or use an aluminum bat to end a conversation.

He had a bachelor pad on the west side. I knocked a few times. No one answered at first, and I took out my pad to write him a note. The chain unlatched and the door opened. He nodded and led me in.

"Sorry to pop in, I figured you would be out of town. Didn't think anybody stayed in the city this late in August who didn't have to."

"I'm between vacations."

We shook hands. He closed the book he was reading and put it off to the side. His apartment was palatial with strange decorations. I guess you call that décor.

"This place is a real shit hole, Sammy. You better try and get out of the lease."

"It's funny you should say that. I was just thinking the same thing."

"I'm sure women will be repulsed. Such filth."

"My accent makes up for it."

"I'm always saying the same thing."

"Take a seat. How have you been?"

"Still above ground"

"I like your optimism. It's impressive; you maintaining that optimism after all the unseemly situations you have managed to get yourself into."

"You got me into a few of those unseemly situations."

"You were out to make a buck and I was out to save my neck."

"Might've been the other way around, but who remember the details."

"Anyways, it is good to see you. It's been years. So why the happy surprise?"

"I though I'd cash in a marker."

"Well you have a few of those with me. Do I need my checkbook?"

"Nope. I caught a case this morning; a case about Michael Lawson. He disappeared or dropped off the radar about six years ago."

"Michael Lawson? I know a Leo Lawson."

"His son"

"Of course. What do you want to know?"

"I've got some miscellaneous shit that I'm starting to link together and I've got a basic timeline. What I'm looking for is some dirt to give him a third dimension. Rumors, whispers, old tales of sorrow and woe, anything you can think of, anything that can make him jump off the page and give me a hint as to where he may have gone."

"Okay. You'll have to bear with me here--But firstly, you look thirsty?"

"I was born that way.

"A stern drink for a stiff detective"

"Yeah. They still help me listen."

His place was modern. It was unfamiliar. Everything in the house was there for display purposes. It was white and shiny. I felt like I was going to smudge everything I went near. He had all his liquor pushed back behind baking goods in a far cabinet in the corner of his kitchen.

"Nice liquor cabinet"

"I took some good advice and gave up drinking."

"Did ya? Gone out of style has it?"

"It hasn't. My antics had."

"Yeah. So you've given up on all liquids, all together or just the good ones?"

"Just the alcoholic ones"

"Yeah. Those would be the good ones."

"I ran into some problems I couldn't fix with a call to my handy private investigator."

"I don't know about that. I can do just about anything. You used to have that huge wine cellar at your old place. Did you keep it?"

"No, I gave it up. Now I just keep a bottle or two for cooking and these dusty liquors for my impromptu guests."

Thankfully, he poured my drink quickly and lavishly. I toasted myself. Halfway through my first gulp, he interrupted me.

"Have you seen her recently? I heard, of course, and was--"

"No."

"She called me a while ago."

"Really?"

"Months at this point, it was the beginning of the summer. She asked to stay at the villa. She was in France at the time. I never use the house in the summer, so I told her she could stay as long as she liked. She said she had come back to the city once or twice. I assumed that--Well who am I to assume?"

"No, she didn't stop in. But that explains a few things."

"Like what?"

I took a large slug of my drink and cracked my neck.

"French and Spanish country codes on my caller ID."

"So you have been talking?"

"She's been calling. We haven't been talking much. I don't want to bore you. Lawson, you said?"

"Right. Yes. Yes. Leo Lawson's boy. Well, I guess he's about--what 35 now?"

"33 in November"

"Let's see. He was studying art for sometime. He sculpted. Attempted to make it into the scene, but his work was too processed."

"He was bad?"

"Bad suggests malice in his work. Well, point in fact there was a bit of malice in his work."

"He was very bad?"

"I'm being too critical. It was ordinary. He was ordinary. He never would have been able to support himself as an artist. Leo knew that. I'm sure he tried to set Michael up with a job. But you know how fathers and sons are. It's all about where the foot prints lay."

"There's a record of Michael working for his father from about '93 to '96 but nothing after that. Do you think he got another job or--"

"Oh no, I am fairly certain that Leo has been his sole means of survival. Leo's well off. Not a particularly warm human being, nor particularly fun, but Leo Lawson is an... adept businessman and wealthy because of it."

"Adept, huh? "

"Quite. The boy stopped going to school and Leo probably saw his son's future long before his son. He must've anticipated a loss with this particular investment, but I know him to be decent. And he's rich enough to flip the bill with a smile for his only son."

"But the kid is a fuck up."

"I thought I was a harsh critic. Lawson just strikes me as the kind of guy who accepts that children are an expense. It's the way of the world. Elizabeth--"

"Elizabeth?"

"Mrs. Leo Lawson. The tougher of the two, undoubtedly."

"Any skeletons in their closet?"

"Nope. Hard to believe, but true. I've met the man. He's a proper snob; greedy and smart. I'm not sure if the business with his daughter gave him a better wrap or a worst wrap."

"Do tell"

"I thought you just wanted to know about the boy."

"Knowing about the girl works too."

"His daughter...Helen, Hera--"

"Heather"

"Yes, Heather. Something of a tom cat, good looking."

"Promiscuous?"

"To say the least. She would get picked up for drugs, alcohol, sex... You name it. She was trying to be a model at some point. Cocaine and runways. That didn't last. Then the partying got a hold, and no one would hire her even with her last name. As I heard it, the legal fees continued

21

to sky rocket and so did the tension between Heather and her mother."

"Because of what? The hard living?"

"The drugs, her friends, the arrests, the instability, the publicity, everything. I don't know. Pick your favorite."

"Between the two of us, the little angel hired me to find her brother."

"Can't say that comes as too much of a shock. She was excommunicated. Elizabeth got fed up. She told her husband to choose: wife or daughter."

"That's some ultimatum."

"Undoubtedly. Either Leo's heart or his pocketbook made him side with his wife. A divorce would have been wildly expensive; while his daughter... like I said, he's a good businessman. He knew when to give up on a lost venture."

"So you think her cut her out just like an extraneous expense?"

"I'm not sure he didn't throw her a few dollars here and there, but for the most part I would think that was it. Lawson knew what was on the line. Heather was crazy. A liability. Like your horses that don't run."

"When was this?"

"Long time. Has to be eight years, now."

"The mother and Heather still don't speak?"

"Well, no."

"Certain?"

"Death is pretty certain."

"Mother's dead?"

"She died a few weeks ago. It was in The Times."

"Must have missed it. Jesus, I've been on the fucking computer all day and I didn't come across anything about his wife dying. Shows you how good I am at using those things."

"I can barely find the internet. My assistant and kids do everything for me. I still have a type writer for God's sake."

"My secretary functions the same way, when she's functioning."

"We are relics from another age."

"I am. You, I'm not so sure. You look more modern than I do. Does anything come to mind about Michael Lawson around the spring of 2001 or afterwards?"

"2001? Before 9/11. Abroad maybe. I really don't know."

"Okay. Traveling."

"Possibly"

"Hey, I appreciate it."

"No, don't mention it. I still have a bunch of markers with you. This was nothing. I am sorry that I wasn't much help. Michael was the child that you didn't hear much about. He wasn't likely to stir up any trouble. Nobody noticed him."

"Thus the case."

"You should go see a friend of mine, if you want to find out more about the Lawson's."

"Who's that?"

"His name is Charlie Goldstein. He shares a lot of friends with the Lawson's. Let me find his number for you."

We both hunched over his computer in the corner of the room. He had his glasses and I was squinting. After minutes of searching and Sam cursing in Spanish we found it.

"Ah... Write this down on your little pad: 169 7th Avenue. Goldstein Design or something like that. I would recommend your pop-in method. If you call him he isn't likely to give you the time of day. But if you show up with a card and an attitude, he'll eat you up."

"Okay. Who is he?"

"He's a gossip. Someone you meet around town. I warn you, he will talk your head off. No one can keep up with him."

"Yeah, but I'll give it a try. He's a rich guy?"

"He's wealthy. Nothing too shocking, but his hobby is high end, socialite gossip. I have no idea how he fits all the information into his pea sized head, but he does."

"I'll look him up."

"Would you like a refill?"

"A quick one, then I should be going."

"Fine"

"Are your kids all grown up now?"

"You could say that. One is 35. One is 33. One is 30. One is 22. One is 20 and one is 16. I think the 16 year old is the most grown up and the 35 year old is the least."

"Six kids, man. I had forgotten it was that many."

"Six children, five wives and I'll probably add some more before I'm done."

"Ha-ha. What the hell is wrong with you? I'm tired just listening to you talk about it. I don't even want to imagine what you pay in alimony and child support."

"It's nothing trivial, believe you me. But luckily I discovered the art of the prenuptial agreement with wives three, four and five."

"A cautious romantic. Which one was Mary?"

"Which number wife? Wife number two, she was the only one that I had a pleasant divorce with. We were both cheating on each other so heavily that the marriage dissolved...organically. Neither one of us wanted the other, so we split up. And then there was the happily ever after. You said she still calls?"

"Yeah. She calls. I don't pick up. But she calls."

"You never pick up?"

"Not ever."

"Why not?"

"I figure when or if she really wants to talk, she knows where to find me."

"Both of you are stubborn. I can't say I am surprised. A standoff is exactly what I would imagine in a fight between you two."

"A standoff is what we've got."

"How long has she been gone?"

"A little over two years"

"Wow. That is strange. If she calls me again and says something, I'll tell her to call you first."

"Too kind. Not sure it matters much at this point. I'd probably just ask her to sign the divorce papers."

"That's too bad. I thought you two had a chance. I mean she did leave me for you. So there must've been some allure."

"Maybe once. Good to see you. Good luck with the kids and the computer."

"Give me a call sometime. We'll find some new women. We're both due."

"Ha-ha. Right."

"See Charlie."

"I will."

"But watch out. He bites."

"Okay."

"And Graves, watch out for Heather Lawson. She fucks."

"Eloquent"

"Watch yourself."

"You know me, Sammy. I'm made of steel." I shook my empty glass at him, handing it over with a grin.

"She might've scored some kryptonite."

I left the apartment glad to escape. Sam knew good and well that I didn't like talking about Mary, and he knew exactly how long she'd been gone. Most people had given up asking about her. That was precisely what I wanted. But I knew he'd bring it up. I was the man she was fucking around with while they were married and now, though we were friends of sorts, I could tell he was getting some satisfaction out of my predicament. She leaves him; he continues to live in the lap of luxury and moves onto the next marriage. Mary leaves me; I continue to live poorly and chase down leads for an excommunicated cokehead. Some guys really are better off.

CHAPTER THREE

I needed another drink after leaving Sam's. Leon's Bar and Grill was two blocks down from my apartment. Robby was tending.

"How's it going, Graves?"

"Today was a pretty good day. How 'bout yourself?"

"Same old shit."

"Double"

"Tough day?"

"They're all tough one way or another."

"That fat guy, Sharpe, was in here yesterday. He find you?"

"Yeah. I'm lucky he didn't eat me."

"Big marker?"

I nodded. I cracked my neck. "The nerve of the Orioles to loose in the 11th and my ponies to all run like fat fourth graders."

"Ponies are bad news, man. Ya know Leon almost lost the bar because of 'em."

"What a loss that would've been."

"Yeah. You'd be heartbroken for sure. You know there was another guy in here earlier looking for you too?"

"Who?"

"Not sure. Some kid."

"What'd he say?"

"I don't know."

"Care to elaborate at all?"

"You're the detective."

"Everyone keeps telling me that."

"He sounded like he was going to come back some time."

"Good, I won't have to waste my evening slummin' in this dump."

"If you think this place is such a fucking dump, why do you keep coming back?"

"Your booze doesn't taste as watered down as the other place I go."

"Graves, how many places do you have in this part of town? You live three blocks away."

"My place is the other place."

"You're pathetic."

"Another thing everyone keeps telling me."

"Another drink?"

"Nah. I think I'll save my dough and head to my other joint. Do me a favor, though, if that kid comes in later give me a call."

"Yeah. Sure. You think he's trouble?"

"Me? I'm usually the last one to know if I'm in trouble. Let me know if you find out."

"Yeah. See ya, Graves."

My apartment was in better shape 10 years ago when my wife bought it. Once I moved in with her, the place took a turn for the worse. It was a nice two bedroom in desperate need of cleaning and a woman. I wasn't a slob. There weren't any old pizza boxes and shit lying around. The apartment just looked worn. Dust covered most of it. I didn't stray much from two or three key stations in the apartment. Most of the life was sucked out of it when Mary left. The pans were never clean, the coffee was always running out and the booze was always over stocked.

I wasn't lonely, but I was alone. It was a solitary existence. The routine was what I hated. I took off my suit coat. I put it over the chair. I meticulously emptied my pockets onto a table next to the door. I checked the fridge. I sighed. There was just no abandoning any of it. Eventually, every night's routine centers around one bottle or another.

I sorted through four or five glasses before I held one up to the light and didn't see grimy shit. I wandered over to the couch, put the bottle to my right and the glass to my left. I turned on an old movie and passed out before I could figure out which one it was.

I woke up too early, and sweaty. I was upright by 8:45, done with my morning routine by 9:15 and picking up a paper outside my office by 9:30. I like perfectly ordinary workdays. They're my favorite. I despise domestic routines, but I cherish vocational routines. I was thoroughly irritated when I saw four uniforms hanging around my office.

"You guys better have a fucking warrant!"

"There was a break in."

"Yeah. I fucking bet."

The patrolman recognized me. He held out his arm. He didn't smile at me. He smiled at the state of my office. He must have known me.

"Pretty simple b and e."

"God-fucking-forbid it get complicated."

The office had been ransacked. They had tossed some shit around and there were papers scattered all over. The waiting area and Renee's desk looked untouched. Another uniform approached me and said, "Graves?"

"Yeah. That's me."

"Hollister. Looks like you had a break in."

"It appears so."

"We got the call about 30 minutes ago. The perp must

have wrecked the door jam and had his way with your office. He probably came in overnight. Anyways, you had better inventory anything you think might be missing. It looks like they mainly focused on your office."

The drawers to all my file cabinets had been opened with a crowbar. My little safe was safe. My workup on Michael Lawson was still perfectly laid out on my desk. The bottom desk drawer was jimmied open. The holster was empty. The Glock, two extra clips and a box of ammunition comprised the full heist.

"Hey--uh. Hollister, right?"

"Yeah"

"I had a gun in this locked drawer. And now I don't." I held up the empty holster.

"Shit."

"Shit is right."

"We'd better go down to the precinct."

"Yes, we had better do that."

"Anything else gone?"

"They got the gun. What else would they want?"

The break-in was meant to be quick. It was quick. They didn't have time to get to the safe or pry open most of my cabinets. They were in a hurry, or they were stupid or once they got the gun they were content. There was no style, no intelligence and no point aside from the acquiring my firearm. I was dealing with a specially educated kind of criminal.

Walking out with Hollister, I found Renee on the stairs.

"Graves, damn it. I told you the IRS would come eventually. I told you--"

"Somebody or bodies broke in."

"Good. It will all be tainted evidence then. Plus it's almost been seven years since--"

"No. Somebody broke in and stole my gun."

"Oh shit. It's not the taxes."

"No"

"It could be worse. Your gun could've been seized by

the IRS."

"I have to go file some papers at the precinct."

"I'm sorry. I'll call a locksmith."

"Yeah. Good idea. I'll be back in a while."

We began to walk down the stairs. Hollister held back to watch Renee walk down the rest of the hall. "She looks like one fine secretary." I cracked my neck and tried to bit my tongue. He saw my expression and apologized.

"Hey, you can't help it. You're a piece of shit."

The station wasn't much different than the last time I had been in there. It was your ordinary shit hole. I filed my report and tried to slip out unnoticed. I knew a lot of the guys in that house. It is a big deal, having a gun stolen, especially if you're a cop. Since I was already a dinger of an embarrassment and a former cop, I opted to not give a shit. But I didn't like the idea of my piece becoming a journeyman of the streets. I didn't like the idea of the cops coming at me if the piece was used. And most of all, I didn't like the idea of staring down the barrel of my ex-property in the near future.

The desk sergeant was an old friend. I stopped by on my way out to have a quick chat.

"Bobby. Bobby, you deaf fuck. Look left."

"Graves. How you doing?"

"Still above ground"

"I can't believe I'm seeing you in a police precinct. You'd think a man might hold a grudge; show a little resentment for previous employers that dumped you 9 weeks short of a pension."

"I'm indifferent towards the world, Bobby. Why would I treat the old boss in blue differently?"

"Ha-ha. How's the 'being a dick' business?"

"Fantastic. You enjoy being a desk sergeant?"

"Old age and arthritis, you know."

"I wouldn't know. Me, I'm stuck at 35. Same clothes, same great shape, same everything. Time can't keep up."

"Maybe when you marry rich. You still with her?"

"More or less. You? Family good?"

"My oldest just graduated from the academy."

"No shit, you didn't feel it was good paternal advice to warn him against it?"

"The girl's stubborn."

"Girl? My lord, I was surprised to hear you could procreate. And a girl to boot. Shit, Bobby 'Doughnuts' having a daughter is--"

"You stay the fuck away from her. 30 years isn't even a fucking big enough gap for her to be safe from you."

"I have a feeling she's safe. Hey, I feel like the streets safer already. Did you hear about my little break in?"

"I just came on. What happened?"

"Some punks took my gun."

"That's terrible. I guess all those years of policing and getting criminals off the street really paid off."

"I blocked all those years out of my memory, Bobby. Too painful. Anyway, I should--"

"Hey, while I got you here, I got a story for you."

"Yeah?"

"Yeah. Two weeks ago my daughter's up in your old part of town, on patrol, and she sees three guys going at this fire hydrant."

"Going at it?"

"It was like 105 degrees. Hot as hell. And these punks, not even kids, fucking imbeciles, are going after this fire hydrant. They can't get it."

"It ain't so easy these days."

"It's a huge fucking mess and everybody hates it. Fucking bravest are up our ass all the time about 'em. Anyways she and her partner pull over and tell 'em to fuck off. They don't even pat 'em down or nothing. They just say 'We're rolling back in an hour and if this thing is going off, you're gonna get--"

"Right"

"As they're giving this fucking speech to these idiots, they turn around and see that right in front of their squad car some dumb fuck has picked up the tools and is going at the hydrant."

"Ha-ha. Jesus."

"They turn around give 'em the 'eh what the fuck'. Guess who it is?"

"Regis Philbin?"

"Benny C."

"My boy, Benny?"

"None other"

"Shocking. Was it that hydrant right outside his parents restaurant?"

"Yeah"

"People are unbelievable. I first caught him doing that shit when he was thirteen. His position in the drug rackets has improved but apparently the mush in his skull hasn't."

"Some people, huh?"

"That dumb motherfucker makes me embarrassed to call myself human. Proof positive that we share ninety-six percent of our genes with chimps. I'll see ya, Bobby. Watch out for those doughnuts."

"Piss off, Graves."

Bobby was grabbing at his big belly and huffing. He grunted and groaned. I chuckled to myself.

The locksmith was working on the office door. Renee was resting on the couch.

"You're back!"

"Relieved or surprised?"

"Relieved. You have to write him a check."

"Right. How much is it going to be?"

"I don't know"

The locksmith managed to blurt out, "I'll be done in a minute."

I had Renee pick up her leg and I sat on the couch. She threw her legs on my lap.

"Tired?"

"I hate cops."

"Probably shouldn't have been one, then huh? Did

they rough you up?"

"Go to dinner with me tonight."

"No."

"Come on."

"No. I can't."

"You've got to eat, right? And he won't eat with you. It'll be an excuse to eat with an actual human being."

She curled in her legs and sat up, noticeably unhappy with the turn in the conversation.

"I'm not going to dinner with you. And I will be having dinner with my husband."

"You being serious?

"Yes, Graves."

"All right"

"Yeah"

"Okay"

"Sign a check and leave."

"I guess my day's over then. Where do you keep them?"

"Top left drawer"

I got the checkbook, and tried as slyly as possible to retrieve the photographs and my notepad.

"Who should I make it out to, buddy?"

"DeLacosse Locksmiths."

"Be gentle with the price. I'm a mostly out of work detective."

I stood in the doorway as the locksmith finished. I handed Renee the check. She made sure to ignore me.

"I need two keys. One for beauty and one for the beast over there."

"Good 'cause I only got two keys."

The locksmith slammed his toolbox and stood up with two keys in his hands. I put one in my pocket and neatly placed the key next to her on the sofa. I cracked my neck and turned to hear the locksmith ask me quietly, "Hey, do you--you do things with wives?"

"Almost exclusively"

"Like following her around and stuff?"

"Talk to my secretary. We'll give you an appointment and the working man special."

"Thanks."

I made it home to do my routine; I took off my jacket, plugged in my cell phone, and then fell onto the sofa. The sofa smelled bad. It smelled like I had slept on it, fully clothed and sweaty the night before. I was pouring a drink and thinking about getting something to eat when the phone rang.

"Yeah"

"Hey, it's Robby. That kid just walked in. He asked if you'd been in again."

"Right. Is he a big guy?"

"Big? No, he's small. He's jittery. He doesn't look like he wants trouble."

"Okay. I'll be down in a bit. Do me a favor and have the chef throw on a steak and potato for me."

"Sure thing"

I clicked the off button and threw the phone into the couch. Gulping down the last of my whiskey, I got to my feet.

"Little jittery man wants to see me, little jittery man gets to see me."

I poured a refill. Drained the glass and slammed it down on the table in the hall. My keys slid off the table as I palmed them on my way out the door. I rolled down my sleeves. It was dusk. People were starting to crowd the streets heading home. I threw open the door to Leon's and entered. Robby was at the other end of the bar, but he gave me a nod as I entered. I sat at the beginning of the bar, away from most of the other patrons. Robby grabbed a Styrofoam box from behind the door to the kitchen. Placing it down in front of me he whispered, "He's in the corner booth."

"Okay."

"Seventeen bucks"

"Seventeen? Jesus. Is that negotiable?"

"No. And don't go starting anything in here either?"

"Who me? There's your lousy seventeen bucks. And here's another couple for your overpriced whiskey. You're depriving my children of an inheritance, you know."

"You don't have kids."

"Yeah. But if I did have kids, would you still be charging me seventeen dollars for a slab of beef?"

"Yes I would."

"That's what I thought."

The kid in the corner was paying attention to the end of my little conversation. When we made eye contact for the first time he jerked his head back down to stare at his glass. He looked up again as I slid in the booth.

"How goes it?"

"Okay. I guess."

"You aren't sure? Shit kid, 'Okay' is already a pretty ambiguous term as is and you not even being sure if you are, in the general sense, 'Okay' is a disturbing thought to me."

"Okay. I am Okay."

"Wonderful. Look at this, you've only known me for ten seconds and we're already building a rapport."

"What do you want?"

"I heard you wanted something from me."

"No"

"Do you know who I am?"

"No"

"You weren't asking to see Graves?"

"No"

"No?"

"I have no idea what you're talking about, Mister."

"None? See my friend Robby over there gave me the heads up that some squirrelly, sullen nobody came in asking for me. Now that, in and of itself, is pretty innocent because a whole bunch of people know this is my regular spot, but even an innocent attempt to find me does make me wonder who wants me found. So once again, what do you want?"

"I--You got the wrong guy."

"Pick up a new gun recently? Do a little redecorating at an office?"

"You got the wrong guy, man."

"My mistake"

"No problem"

"You in a hurry? Stick around, and I'll buy you a drink. That is of course if you are of age."

"Thanks, but I gotta go."

"Sure thing. Adios."

He awkwardly hustled out from his side of the booth, and then from the bar. I sat in the booth for a couple of seconds, wondering what he was up to. I wasn't too concerned because the kid seemed jumpy and feeble. I thought he might be a cheating wife's tamed tail looking to give me a piece of her mind. I wasn't really nervous. But it had started me thinking and I had started drinking. As my thoughts circulated and wandered, I smelled the kid's drink. I took a sip. It was just soda. I nearly gagged. I got up from the booth and waved to Robby. I got out a couple more bucks and threw it down on the bar.

"Might as well do one more."

He poured. I drank. We chatted. I cracked my neck. I walked out with my dinner already cold.

I made it to the second floor before I started checking my pockets to remember which one I had stashed my keys in. I checked my right and left pant's pocket, then my back pockets and my shirt pocket. My first attempts failed. Then I tapped my right leg again, threw my right hand into the pocket and pulled out my keys. Balancing the Styrofoam in my left hand, I singled out the key to my apartment in my right hand.

Then I heard it. In all the time I've been above ground, I've heard millions of sounds. Gunshots, bone breaks, car crashes, car horns, slurps, shouts. You name it, and, like most people, I've heard it. And I don't spook easily. Aside from gunshots and nails on a chalkboard, you aren't going to get me to flinch. But I will tell you now that when I heard a faint exhalation and a simultaneous creek as I put my key to the door, I spooked. It was the sound you hear before you get hit by something you don't see coming. But I may have been extra jumpy because I was drunk.

I didn't hear him take steps towards me. I could sense that he was hiding on the landing between my floor and the next. I got flustered and tried to open the door in a rush. But of course I dropped my food. In a feeble attempt to grab the falling container, I got distracted. The shadowy figure emerged quicker than I expected. He approached, and I reacted. I heard him mutter, "Graves".

It was too late. He had his arm out stretched. I slapped it away, thinking he had a knife. I wrestled him down to the floor. It wasn't a pretty battle. I was no Ali. He was no Frasier. I snuck in a punch or two. He swatted at me. When all was said and done, we were both panting but I had my knee on his back. The kid was on his stomach. He was wheezing nearly as hard as I was.

"Ah--What--what the fuck are you trying to do?"

"Get off me"

"Tell me what the fuck you're doing here."

"I needed to talk with you somewhere else. You're crushing my chest."

I flipped the guy over. He was the kid from Leon's.

"Fuck, kid. Didn't your mother ever teach you not to sneak up on people?"

"I wasn't sneaking up on you. You're drunk."

"Who are you?"

"Paul Jensen. I think you broke my ribs."

"What do you want?"

"I need to talk to you."

"We're already talking, dip shit. Spit out what you want."

"Give me a second. I didn't expect to be attacked."

"What were you expecting? A hug?"

"Heather Lawson."

"What about her?"

"I think you broke one of my ribs."

"Shit, well you ruined my steak. Come on in."

I finished turning the key and picked up the overturned Styrofoam box. We went into the apartment.

"What do you want with Heather Lawson?"

"She hired you, right?"

"I don't discuss who does or doesn't--"

"I need to find her."

"Good luck"

"Please, you have no idea what I've been through. Just tell me where she is. Okay?"

"I can't do that."

"Shit, man. My chest is killing me. ...You ever had a really bad day?"

"One? No, I usually get like a string of really shitty ones in a row."

"I'm on about my twentieth bad day in a row."

"You want a glass of water?"

"Yeah"

I went into the kitchen, looked at all the seemingly clean but truly dirty glasses and then reached for a coffee mug in the cabinet. I waited a few seconds, rolling my head around making loud cracking noises. I filled the mug twice for myself then filled it up a third time for Paul.

"Here ya go"

"Thanks. You want to know why I'm looking for her?"

"Not really."

Defeated, the kid slumped back into his chair.

"Come on, man. Help me out here. I need to find her because she owes this guy a lot of money and if he doesn't get it soon they're going to take it out on me. And I have a daughter and a girl friend, man. You know?"

"Who does she owe?"

"A bad guy. It doesn't matter."

"It probably does. I don't like competition when it comes to who gets paid."

"Unless you make like 10 grand an hour I don't think there will be any fucking competition, man. Tell me where she is. No one has to get hurt. You can just tell me and then it will all be over."

"Who's going to get hurt? Who said anything about anybody getting hurt, Paul? Because if you're here to make some--"

"No, man. No. I mean she owes a lot. Okay?"

"I believe you. So how much and to whom?"

"Man, you don't want to know."

"I do if they're gonna get in the way of me getting paid."

"I can pay you more than she will, if you just tell me where she is. I swear."

"I'll deliver her for 5 grand."

"Okay. Where is she?"

"Calm down. She gave me a cell phone number."

"No, man. I have her fucking cell phone number. But it's not like she's going to just pick it up."

"She will for me."

"She won't. Fuck."

He threw his glass down. He was nearly shivering as he abruptly headed for the door.

"Here, take this. It's my card. It's got all my numbers and the address of my office."

"I don't need your card."

"I don't think you know what you need."

"I can't, man. If he even knows I was here talking to you, he'll break my legs or do something fucking retarded."

"Who the fuck are you so scared of?"

"Ha-ha. I've got to go, Detective Graves."

"Take the card."

He obliged. As soon as he had it in his pocket, he walked off. It's hard to instill that kind of fear in a person, even a kid. Heather owing big didn't surprise me. It worried me. It also pissed me off. It meant I was going to have trouble getting money out of her when the time came. Worst of all it meant that this case wasn't going to be as simple as finding Michael Lawson.

I hate mysteries. That's what I thought as I slouched down in the couch watching television later that night. I could sense the quicksand lurking. It was waiting for me to take one unsuspecting step, so it could tow me under. My thoughts were wandering. My blood pressure and blood alcohol were rising. Beating up on the kid had made me feel a bit melancholic. I wanted to apologize to someone. So I called Renee.

"Hello"

"Hey, it's me."

"What?"

"You know, you win. I'm sorry."

"About what?"

"Being an ass earlier."

"I've gotten used to that."

"I'll get you an air conditioner. I don't want you to be uncomfortable. And I wasn't trying to force you into dinner. He's a great guy sometimes and you guys need to have dinner together. ...But you know I was just thinking that you need to get out from underneath this prick. He's really no good. A huge--"

She hung up. I shook my head and redialed. I muttered, "Everybody always hangs up on me" as I finished the glass next to my couch.

"I'm sorry, but--"

"Graves, you're being an asshole now. You are obviously drunk. You need to shut up."

"Why? Is he there?"

"No. Thankfully, he's out."

"Thankfully? Ha-ha. Exactly. You don't want him around."

"I don't want him around when you're drunk dialing

me?"

"Drunk dialing?"

"Graves, what are you trying to do here? You're my boss. This is my personal life you're butting into."

"Well, he doesn't deserve you. And-- I'm more than just your boss."

"Graves--"

"What I've been meaning to say to you is that... I think he is a bad husband and--"

"Shut the fuck up, Graves. You're pissing me off. You have no idea what you're talking about."

"Renee, the guy is a pompous dick."

"Are you through?"

"Okay. But this ass hole doesn't even let me call you on the house phone?"

"Because you broke his hand!"

"He broke his own hand. I just helped him fall. And as I recall, I wouldn't even have made him fall on his hand if he--"

"Our issues are exactly that. Ours. It's a husband and wife thing, Graves. Husband and wives are the ones that work it out. Not washed up, liquor soaked detectives."

"Okay"

"You wouldn't know, because no woman ever bothered to try and work shit out with you."

"Right. Thank you for the reality check."

"I shouldn't have said that. That was mean. It's just that he is my husband, Graves. I do love him."

"You do not."

"For all his faults, I do. He's not perfect. Neither am I. But what we have is worth sticking around for. Good night, Graves."

"Are you going to come to work tomorrow?"

"...We'll see."

Renee hung up. I rolled my head around, cracking my neck multiple times.

"That backfired."

CHAPTER FOUR

I passed out watching baseball on the couch. I woke up the next morning around 9:30. I got to the office around 10:15. The outer office door was locked. I sighed in agony as I reached into my pockets to retrieve my new key. Renee wasn't there. Starting shit the night before was a mistake. I figured she wanted some space, but I hoped she'd be back by midday. Around 11:30, I gave Pierce a call. I was bored, and he always went for lunch at 11:30.

"How's it going?"

"Terrible. How's the private sector?"

"Desolate. You got nothing to look forward to once you give up on the job. Well, there was the b and e."

"I heard."

"I'm glad my misfortune has hit the rumor mill."

"So who did it, super dick?"

"Don't know."

"Who wants to steal your gun?"

"I can think of about three hundred different fucking characters. I've got another name I want you to run through B.C.I."

"Look at your watch, Graves."

"I'm aware it's Lieutenant Champlain's lunch hour. I

42

was hoping the lieutenant would run the name when he returned to his cubicle."

"I don't even know why I do this anymore. You ran out of favors long ago."

"Paul Jensen. He's young, mid twenties probably. Look for drug busts, petty shit."

"A regular punk. Okay. I'll run him through when I get back. I'll call you later in the afternoon."

"Why don't we meet for a cup of coffee?"

"I could probably pull that off around 3."

"I'll come down to 1 PP."

"Why don't we just meet at the place that you like? The one that's--"

"Embarrassed to be seen with me around Police Plaza?"

"Yes"

"Call my phone before you leave."

"Yeah. Yeah."

Before I hung up, I heard knocking at the outer office door.

"Come in"

He either didn't hear me or didn't want to enter. He stood there as I yelled again for him to enter. I got up and opened the door to the scouring face of Benny C.

"How ya doing, Detective Graves?"

"My God"

"Mind if I come in?"

"Absolutely. Do not take another step or I'll have you fucking arrested."

"You can't do that. You aren't a cop anymore. Besides, I have a legitimate reason for coming."

"There isn't a legitimate bone in your body."

"But I'm a potential client. Doesn't that mean anything?"

"I have qualifications for my clients. They have to be able to read, sign their name, write a check, not have been convicted of multiple felonies, not be a drug runner... You don't meet the criteria."

"Five grand. Completely legit. Look at this place, you've got to be interested?"

"Not one bit. Get out of my fucking building."

"You not being a cop no more makes your threats less scary."

"Is that so?"

"Yeah"

"You been here before?"

"No"

"Didn't pick up some new hardware in this neighborhood the other day?"

"I don't know what you're talking about."

"I think you got an idea."

"Back off, like I said you aren't so scary without a badge. You're just a guy."

"You're wrong. I'm much scarier as a private dick."

"I don't think so."

"But I am. Because I'm still mean and now, I hit civilians."

"What--"

I hit him squarely in the nose with a quick jab. "Don't bleed in my hallway."

I slammed the outer office door a few inches from his face. I hurried back to my own office, cursing and realizing I had no gun in the office. I thought about grabbing an umbrella but remembered I had a bat in the corner of my office. I grabbed the bat and put it next to my desk. I felt assured he wasn't coming back after that humiliation. I expected him to admit defeat and walk away. That would've been the smart thing to do. Of course, he wasn't smart. He knocked on the door again.

"Benny, if you come through that fucking door and you're packing, so help me--"

"I'm not here to fuck with you. All I want is to hire you. I'll give you five grand for this bitch. And you already know where she is."

"I told you I didn't want your money. You should work on your listening skills."

"Two minutes, Graves. You could make five grand in cash in two minutes. Money is money."

"Thank you for clearing that up for me."

He entered hesitantly. Benny had one hand on his bleeding nose and his other resting by his side.

"How's the nose?"

"Fucking broken. The deal is you tell me where I can find Heather Lawson and I give you five thousand dollars in cash."

"Heather Lawson?"

"Yes"

"I told your guy last night I didn't know."

"What guy?"

"Jensen. Paul Jensen"

"….I don't know no Paul Jensen."

"You don't know no Paul Jensen?"

"Nah, never heard of him. What did he ask you to do?"

"He wanted the same thing you want."

"That's a coincidence."

"Is it?"

"I think so."

"She must be a popular girl. She's got guys looking for her all over town."

"Yeah. She's hot."

"So why do you want her?"

"Five large. How 'bout an address?"

"What did Jensen tell you I said?"

"Look he--I told you I don't know Jensen."

"Right and you're full of shit."

"You want the money or what?"

I wanted the money. I needed the money. Plus, taking money from Benny C. would be easy and fulfilling. I had no intention of actually giving her up. He was just my favorite kind of idiot to swindle.

"Three grand now and two grand when I find her."

"What?"

"It's called a retainer, shit head. I just don't go running off with my dick waving in the wind. You have to pay up at the get-go and at the finish."

"I'll give you fifteen hundred now."

"You'll give me three grand now."

"Wait. Why don't you just give me her address and I'll give you all five grand now?"

"I don't have an address. I don't know where she is right now. But I can find her."

"When?"

"Three grand. Now."

"Two grand."

"Three grand or the door"

"Fine. But I know she's been here. You should keep track of the people that you work for."

His gangster roll bulged with at least seven grand.

"What? You're a fucking moron. That's thirty, one hundred dollar bills, Benny. Do you want me to help you count?"

"Fuck you. I lost my place."

"Looks like 'H' is running better than water uptown? Huh?"

After a painful minute, he dropped thirty crisp one hundred dollar bills on my desk. It was Christmas. An ex-con who wouldn't walk into a police station or a courthouse voluntarily if his life depended on it was dropping off three thousand dollars without any documentation or proof of our agreement. It was satisfying and uplifting. Plus as I owed about thirty-seven hundred to Sal and Sharpe, it was good for my health.

Benny left peacefully enough. I put the three grand in my little safe. As I locked it back up, the phone rang. Pierce was ready for his afternoon caffeine fix. I unlocked the safe again, and retrieved two grand. I called Sharpe up.

"Graves. Exactly the man I want--"

"I've got two grand for you."

"I hope you get the additional seventeen hundred before--"

"I'll drop off two grand. Will that get you off my back for a while?"

"It'll buy you a couple of days."

"Okay"

"You coming by now?"

"Yeah. Oh...The Orioles are at the stadium tonight. What's it looking like for the--"

"You got outstanding debts. You don't have money to gamble with until--"

"Well, I don't have the whole thirty seven hundred. I have twenty five hundred. But I need to live on something and if you let me put down say three hundred on the Orioles--"

"No, Graves"

"Well maybe I won't stop by."

"Threatening me by saying you ain't going to pay. That don't make much sense."

"You don't make much sense. You're still getting paid. I'll even give you the three hundo up front."

"Graves. ...Fine"

"Good boy. Sit tight."

I walked out of Sharpe's with a grin and made it down to the coffee shop fashionably late. I spotted Pierce because he was wearing one of his three over worn suits. He looked battered.

"Nice tie"

"Margie gave it to me. It's ...horrific, but if I don't wear it every so often...you know."

"You are a domesticated motherfucker, aren't ya?"

"You wouldn't believe how high the pile of shit is on my desk. This fucking detail is despicable. I've got to deal with FBI, DEA, and IRS motherfuckers. Then on top of everything I got the Port Authority trying to fuck my brain because some ingenious motherfucker keeps trying to make crates go missing. I'm fucking miserable." He drank the coffee as if he hoped I might have spiked it for him.

"Hey, don't pump yourself up to high. You're still a hump in my book."

"The only thing getting me through the days is knowing I'm still so much better off than you."

"Yeah. Being me is so damn good it's a curse."

"Getting involved with a high end, drugged out socialite is a curse."

"Guess who came to my office asking about the socialite."

"I hate when people say that. I know thousands of fucking people out of millions in New York and billions in the world. How the fuck am I supposed to guess one human being that came to your office?"

"Good God, man. Benny C."

"No shit?"

"Knocked on my door and wanted to be treated like a 'legitimate' client. His words, not mine."

"You take a job off him?"

"Kind of, no real intention of following through on it but he did leave a hefty retainer."

"Good, you've robbed him blind. Now all you have to do is beat the shit out of him and you'll probably feel like all is settled."

"Well..."

"Tell me you didn't"

"Before I decided to rob him blind, I was going to settle for a cheap shot. I ended up getting both."

"You're joking."

"I might regret it later but right now I like knowing the fact that he's got a broken nose and I'm three grand richer."

"Incredible. ...What was the job?"

"Guess. Ha-ha." Pierce stood up. "Don't leave, you fuck."

"What's the job?"

"He wants me to find the Lawson girl for him."

"What does Benny C. want with some spoiled heiress?"

"I'll tell ya when I figure that out myself. But knowing Benny, there are very few possible things he wants with her that he'd be willing to pay five grand."

"Five grand. Yeah, he wants some loving, wants her money or her head."

"Yes, to put it in even less unsubtle terms."

"You know the genre of people your dealing with, right?"

"I haven't forgotten."

"I forgot about this. You got me all riled up."

Pierce removed a few pages of white paper folded from his inner coat pocket. The few sheets of paper were Paul Jensen's arrest record and initial coroner report.

"He's dead?"

"Apparently. The coroner's report just came in before I left. He had a few drug collars. He got caught with a few 8 balls, speeding in Brooklyn. Not much else of any merit. He didn't do any time. He got off with a lot of probation. The autopsy will come in a while."

"Probation with that much weight?"

"Rich kid, first time offense and a good lawyer. It's not the hand of God. Garbage man found him early this morning. Close range, automatic, one shell recovered, .40 S and W cartridge."

".40 S and W?" I queried rhetorically, cracking my neck.

"Yeah like from a Glock 22C. You used to own a 22c didn't ya? You used to know this kid, didn't ya?"

"Shit. Yeah, well it was stolen and I'm too lazy to kill anyone."

"That is true."

"Ballistics gotten a match?"

"Graves, he got found this morning."

"Nothing to go on?"

"I didn't call up the lead. But it smells funky."

"I saw this fucking kid last night."

"You did?"

"He followed me into Leon's and then jumped—semi-jumped me outside of my place. He was running from someone."

"Not fast enough. You should call up the lead. Throw him a bone."

"Fuck him"

"You're such a piece of shit. Have you completely forgotten you were ever on the job?"

"I've tried to."

"Who does it say caught it?"

"Investigating officer is one Dante Hope."

"Over in the 15th."

"I assume. Hope… I never heard of this guy."

"Yes, you have. You don't remember Dante Hope?"

"No, should I?"

"Yes, you should. You know, Graves, I don't usually get too concerned throwing you some bullshit here and there--"

"Hey, if you--"

"Let me finish. I don't like this. Uptown broads, drug collars, Benny C, kid who tries jump you ends up dead on arrival. This smells bad, pal."

"I know how it smells. It's just another job with a curious mix of high and low society."

"It's a job that's not worth it."

"I think it might be worth it. You didn't see Benny's face or his gangster roll."

"Graves, I got a shit load of work. Margie's parents are coming into town next week. I need you getting neck high in shit-sand like I need a bullet in the brain. I don't want to be bailing you out."

"Me, the one tangled up in quicksand and needing rescuing?"

"Yeah"

"Right. I'm not involved in anything. I don't care enough. I'm morally askew and you know it. You like quicksand, not me. Like the Simeon thing?"

"Bull shit. You cite that shit every time that you want a favor from me."

"That's right because we weren't supposed to even be fucking involved and then you forgot to check--"

"I did fucking not. I keep telling you, he came out of the bathroom and Sully was supposed--"

"Nah Nah Nah. That isn't--"

"Graves. Fuck you. Okay how about the time in anti-crime and you were working on that numbers scam with that fucking chick."

"Wait. Which chick? The chick I was fucking that was running the numbers scam? Or the chick I was--"

"Yeah. The one you were sleeping with."

"That does not count."

"That counts."

"I was no where near getting tapped during that shit, and I was not neck high in quicksand."

"As I remember it, I had to write a fucking novel after discharging my service revolver three times in the line of duty protecting my pussy chasing partner."

"She wasn't really going to shoot me."

"She was going to shoot you."

"Not fatally. She really liked me."

"Just promise me that you're going to deal with this case like you usually do. You're going to get your money, you're going to do your job as shitty as possible, and you're going to live to see another day."

"Pierce, it isn't that fucking serious. It's a couple of fucking junkies. It's going to take a lot more than some bangers and an uptown socialite to put a scratch on me."

"I'm not buying you being an arrogant smartass today. Use your head. It's quicksand."

"It ain't quicksand if you can see it coming. I can handle this. Don't worry. It makes you look older. Not as old as that tie makes you look, ...but still...I'll see ya."

I headed out of the coffee shop after giving Pierce a

quick pat on the back to lift his spirits. We were good when we partnered up; quick, sharp and as effective as necessary. We've dulled down. He was always good police. I fluctuated. I was stubborn, but I picked my battles. That left me looking for the easy-way-out a lot. Much to the chagrin of I.A.B, my lieutenants and Pierce, I found those easy-ways-out often and easily. I didn't like paperwork or inane bureaucracies or getting taken advantage of by cops or criminals. I always wanted to be the one taking the advantage.

CHAPTER FIVE

Back at the office, a light on the message machine was blinking. I found the playback button eventually. There was only one message. Renee's voice echoed out of the speaker.

"Graves, it's Renee. ...If you get this message--I just wanted you to know that ... I couldn't make it into today. And I may be taking a few days off, but... I'll call you or you can call me if you need me...Bye."

The message tapered out, leaving me feeling exceedingly guilty and annoyed. Her husband held a grudge. He was cheating. Yet, Renee and I were the ones getting punished. And that mattered to me.

"Fuck me"

I threw my suit coat on my desk, cracking my neck in the process. I picked up the baseball bat half considering bringing it with me. Deciding it would be bulky on the subway, I opted to put it back in the corner of the office. The murder of the kid and Benny's visit had me a bit spooked. I seldom carried a gun. But now I wanted to carry one. I could've gone home and grabbed the old .45 that I kept there, but I wasn't about to make that detour for Roberto Carpagni.

I sat on the 1 train, jammed between a fat guy and a young woman singing not so quietly along with her iPod. It was hot. I was sweaty and uncomfortable, shimmying in my seat and gently elbowing the fat guy. He didn't get the message and by 68th street I was standing, judging him silently.

Renee's husband owned a brownstone. Unfortunately for the community, Roberto had made partner his firm. He was in marketing or advertising. I don't know which it was, because I don't know the difference. Either way he had money. Enough money to splurge on Manhattan hotels for midday romps. I rang the bell until she cracked open the door.

"Yes."

"Hey"

"Graves, you--"

"Open the door."

"No"

"I'm sorry. Honestly, please let me in."

Begrudgingly, Renee peeled the door back.

I stepped inside about to launch headfirst into a lengthy apology. "I just wanted to say--"

But when she went to back peddle, she had to clutch the wall. She stood on one foot with swollen knuckles and bruised arms.

"...Because I called."

"Don't be ridiculous."

"Fuck. You're limping. Sit down."

She hobbled to her couch. I found a washcloth near the sink, dampened it, and removed a bag of berries from the freezer. I sat next to her and administered my kitchen aids.

"What happened?"

"I hit him."

"Why?"

"...I had my reasons." She relinquished.

"So then, he hit you back."

"No. Not exactly. I went to hit him again as he was

stumbling, and I fell down the stairs."

"Right" I mumbled, unconvinced.

"I did. He came home at two. He couldn't string a coherent sentence together. And he fell into bed fully clothed and smelling like another woman's perfume."

"Sorry"

"No, you're not. This let's you say all the things you want to say. Don't pity me, Graves. I don't need your pity or your charity."

"Good, because you can't have either."

"So why are you here?"

"You weren't at the office to make me coffee. So I figured you could make me some here--"

"I don't make you coffee. It's not in my job description."

"Yeah. In my experience, it's best to apply the warm compress, and then the cold compress. Then the warm compress again with a stiff drink and so on."

"I get it."

"You only had frozen berries."

"I know."

I pulled off the towel and put the berries against her ankle. Her skin was smooth and her legs were luxurious. I couldn't help but scan them up and down. She caught me of course and asked, "So how does it look?"

Oblivious, I answered "Very nice".

"My swollen ankle looks nice?"

"Eh no. No. It looks fucked up. But--"

"You eying me, Graves?"

"Can't seem to pull 'em away."

She blushed a bit and shook her head. I was beat red. 'Very nice' was a gross understatement, though. From ear to ankle, her body was right in all the right ways. She had the body. She had the loyalty. She had the passion. She had the grace that comes with independence and the allure that comes with strength. As a professional investigator, take my word on this. Renee had it all. Except for a good man.

"Are you going to let me take you to the hospital?"

"No"

"What if I ask politely?"

"Politely? No, maybe if you get a court order or light my drapes on fire or something--"

"There's got to be a match around here somewhere--"

"No. Stop. Because I know you would actually light my drapes on fire, I will go if you beg."

"Never was much for begging. I don't have the knees for it."

"You're impossible. Let me go and change."

The two of us stood on the corner five minutes later. Renee leaned against me as I hailed a cab. My phone went off in the cab. Renee found it in my coat pocket before I did.

"This is Graves."

"It's Pierce. You need to go see the lead that caught that D.O.A. you knew."

"Why?"

"Because it's common fucking courtesy and on top of that he just gave me the heads up that he wanted to see you."

"What'd he say?"

"That you came up in the investigation. I gave him your number. Go by the house--"

"He's at the 15th?"

"Yeah."

"Fuck that. He can come to me."

"Graves, be fucking reasonable. Go down to the one five and save him a trip. He's good police."

"What's his name again?"

"Dante Hope. Tall black guy, sharp. You know him."

"So you keep telling me."

"Go see him."

"I don't have the time."

"You fuck, I'm not playing middleman anymore. Take down his number."

"Uh huh..."

"212-555-1929. Okay?"

"Okay. Got it."

"You didn't even write it down did you?"

"Adios, brother."

I hadn't written it down. I cracked my neck. I hung up.

I waited between a fat guy and old man at the hospital. The old man may have been unconscious and the fat guy was wheezing. I put my finger under the old man's nose to make sure he was still alive. Renee came out on a pair of crutches. A nurse walked along side of her with her purse and some papers.

She nodded towards me and said to the nurse, "He'll carry my purse, thanks."

"Sure. Make sure to keep your weight off that ankle for a few days. Have a good one."

I nodded in appreciation to the nurse as she left. Renee wasn't putting much effort into using her crutches.

"Didn't they teach you how to use those?"

"I expect you can take them and show me how to properly use them."

"I expect I could figure it out."

"They're crutches. There isn't much to figure out."

"You seem to be having a fair amount of difficulty."

"This is how you're supposed to use them."

"No. You're supposed to swing. Rock back and forth."

"You are not."

"Yes, you are"

"That's if you have a broken leg. There's a different method if you've only got a sprained ankle."

"Method? How many schools of thought do you think there are on--"

She swung and hit me in the shin with the crutch before I could finish. Wincing, I posed a question. "Alright. Where to now?"

"A hotel"

"He can call the credit card company and find out what

hotel you're at."

"…Maybe. But he's not much of a detective, Graves."

"…Neither are you. …C'mon. Why don't you come and stay at my place for a while?"

"I don't know."

"There's a spare room. It's that simple. Free, clean and safe… when I'm not there."

"Ha-ha. Just until I work some things out."

"You wouldn't be up for filing some battery charges against him, would you?"

"I'm more worried about him charging me."

"Well, we could lie and beat him to the punch yet again, so to speak."

"Graves, I want you to shut up because I have a little bit of a headache. And other than that I just want you to call me a cab, hold on to my purse and let me rest."

"Okay. You're a cab. Now I'll shut up."

I could see her breaking into a grin as I evaded another crutch to the shin.

"You didn't even think that up. That's from 'Singin' in the Rain'."

"Get in the cab"

We arrived at my apartment building around nine. She had trouble with the stairs.

"Put the weight on your good foot, then bring up the crutches, then--"

She threw the crutches over to me and jumped up the rest of the stairs using the railing for balance.

"Tougher than you look"

"Tougher than you"

"You're pretty good at the whole 'take what I said and throw it back at me' thing."

"You make it so easy"

My cell phone rang. I gave Renee the keys as I held her crutches, purse and my cell phone.

"Yeah. Graves"

"Graves, it's Dante Hope over at the 15th. How's it

going?"

"It goes. How are things at the one five?"

"Not enough time in the day."

"Sure"

"The reason I'm calling is that your name popped up in an investigation and I was wondering if you would stop by the station. Or if it's more convenient we can come by your office tomorrow morning."

"For a change I'm actually fairly busy. Business picked up. Can I clear something up for you over the phone?"

"I just need to grab a quick statement from you."

"Mind telling me why or about what?"

"Fifteen minutes. We'll be in and out."

"11:30 tomorrow. How'd my name come up?"

"With the wind. See you tomorrow Graves."

I put the crutches and purse on the couch. Renee had crashed into the chair. My wallet and keys whirled around the ceramic bowl on the table.

"Who was that?"

"Detective Dante Hope of the 15th precinct."

"What did you do?"

"When I find out, I'll let you know. It has to do with the kid, I'm just not sure how."

"What kid?"

"You're a bit behind aren't ya?"

"Apparently"

"This kid was asking around for me at Leon's. I got a call that he was in, so I went down, spooked him and he ended up...semi-attempting to jump me."

"To mug you?"

"No"

"Where was this?"

"Outside the apartment."

"What did you do to him?"

"Nothing. We...tussled. Anyway, he was asking about our new client, Ms. Lawson. She seems to be entangled in a substantial debt to an unsightly fella."

"Who?"

"The kid, Paul, wouldn't say. But he was scared shitless and he ran off. And he came up to D.O.A. this morning."

"That's terrible. Did you know him at all?"

"Nope, not really"

"You don't seem too broken up about it."

"Like I said, I didn't really know him."

"Still. ...I guess the case isn't as straight forward as you thought."

"Sure it is. I'm getting paid to find Michael Lawson. That is all I intend to do. Nothing more. Nothing less. This other shit is just ...peripheral."

"You think you are going to be able to keep it that simple?"

"...No, but it's always worth a try."

We settled in and Renee looked uncomfortable soon after.

"You're place is just... nasty. There's like a thick coating of dust-- or whatever this substance is--- over everything. You should just burn it down and start over."

"Nah, I like the wallpaper."

"There isn't any wallpaper."

"Oh. There used to be."

The house phone rang. I bitterly muttered, "Where all these fucking phone calls coming from?"

"Welcome to my world."

Renee had her feet up on the coffee table. She was thumbing through a very old issue of Esquire. I had trouble reading the caller I.D. at first. I almost couldn't believe that it read: Chan, Benji. Infuriated, I slapped the 'talk' button.

"Whilst I'm proud that you've mastered the ability to dial phone numbers in spite of your peanut sized brain, I was pretty sure that--"

"Have you found her?"

"No"

"Why not?"

"Because I haven't."

"Have you tried to find her?"

"Sure I have. I've run through everything. Followed up on a hundred leads. Nobody seems to know anything."

"Yeah, man, tell me about it. This fucking slut has completely gone off the radar. We so need to fucking find her."

"We?"

"Look, Graves, we know you must know where she is. She hired you. She was at your office. You had better give her up."

"I don't know where she is, Benny. Why don't you tell me who you're working for these days and then I'll figure out which punks she's trying to hide from and I'll go from there?"

"No. No. No. You just fucking find her."

"Great. Got ya. Bye Benny."

"Tomorrow, Graves. Fucking Tomorrow."

"Benny, the day you give me dead lines is the day I start shitting diamonds."

"I'm paying you."

"Yes. I'm aware."

"You find her or you're going to get fucked, man."

"Ha-ha. First off, fuck yourself. Secondly--"

"Graves, I will be at your office at five tomorrow. You better have something for me."

"Call and make an appointment tomorrow. I have this terrible feeling that my schedule is booked. But since you're a paying and pathetic customer, maybe we can make room. Bye Benny."

I really disliked Benny. I didn't hate him. Hatred is a terrible thing. It clouds one's judgment. But I really disliked him. And a serious disliking can confuse a man. I should never have taken Benny's money. I realized that even before he called me at home. I thought making a buck off his suffering would in some way ease mine. I was confused.

"Who was that?"

"Benny C"

"And who is Benny C?"

"Benny C is a mentally challenged little hood who thinks he's big and bad."

"He's a client?"

"No. I just plain stole his money."

"Isn't that what you do to everyone?"

"No, usually I take with one hand and ask for more with the other."

"That's right. I knew that."

"You'd approve, if you knew Benny. He was one of many local idiots back when I was uptown. He came up in a lot of small time drug bust bullshit. He was lucky, though. He only got busted twice, and he made rank. When he came by the office this morning, I broke his nose and took three grand from him to find Heather Lawson."

"Doesn't that present a conflict of interest?"

"I never had any intention of giving her up to Benny. I just intended to take his money and his pride. But now with this Jensen kid dead I sense that Heather knows she picked the wrong crowd."

"Drug dealers and murderers do tend to be the wrong crowd."

"Indeed."

CHAPTER SIX

I dreamed I was drowning. It may have been a nightmare, but I woke up before I died or survived. So I'm not sure how to qualify it. The door to the spare bedroom was cracked open. I lightly tapped the door to get a better look into the room. Renee was still sleeping. She lay perfectly still. I would've thought she was dead if I hadn't seen her chest move.

I walked down the hall to find a note on the floor. It had been slipped under the door. The stationary was expensive. It was addressed to "Mr. Graves". I knew what it was immediately. I removed the note. It read: "Please come by our apartment whenever you find it convenient. We would like to talk to you. Thank You, Norman and Claudia"

Norman and Claudia lived in the only other apartment on the floor. They were old and talkative, and basically unpleasant for those two reasons. They liked to put notes under my door whenever they wanted something from me.

I showered, shaved, and dressed. I threw my phone, keys, and wallet in my pockets. I grabbed Norman and Claudia's note. Renee emerged from the spare room.

"Good morning."

"Morning."

"You're up early."

"Couldn't sleep any longer, too much rattling around upstairs." I said, shaking my forefinger at my head

"That must be a change of pace."

"Hang around here today. I'm going to talk to this cop and then try and dig myself out of the sandy grave I've walked into."

"I'd rather not. I think I'll--"

"Hold on for just... a few hours. Then we'll finish the argument. Okay? Good."

I stepped out and immediately walked to the apartment across the hall. I knocked and waited. Claudia answered the door.

"Hello, Mr. Graves."

"Hello, Claudia. What can I do for you this morning?"

"Come in. Come in. I'll get you some coffee before you head off to the police station."

"Claudia, I'm not a cop any more. I haven't been for a long time."

"Oh yes. I apologize. Norman! Just one second, Norman will be right here. But come on in. Come in."

"I'd love to, Claudia, but I have to get to work. Is there something you need me for specifically or could the super maybe do it..."

"Oh no, it's nothing like that."

"Of course not--"

"Wonderful. Norman...Mr. Graves is here."

"I am in a rush. Maybe I could stop in some other time."

"That won't work for us."

"Right. So what can I do for you?"

"Norman, come here!" Claudia instructed her husband with frenzied gesticulations. Norman's glasses were hanging on the end of his nose as he appeared in the doorway. He held a paper in one hand and looked remarkably disinterested in seeing me.

"Hello, Mr. Graves."

"Norman, what can I do for you?"

"Well, I have no idea what-- Oh, yes. Claudia... and I were concerned because the other night when we came back from a dinner..."

"Uh huh"

"We saw this strange young man hovering on the landing."

"Yeah, he caught up with me."

"Was he one of those crazy hop heads?"

"We didn't really get to know each other."

"We heard something of a ruckus a bit after we saw him too."

"Yeah. That was when he caught up with me. There's no problem."

"You're sure? Because we don't want any hopheads hanging around the apartment building. It wouldn't be safe."

"He won't be bothering you. I can promise you that. The building is perfectly safe. Bye Claudia. Bye Norman."

"Goodbye, Mr. Graves"

Walking to the office I tried to decide exactly what to give Detective Hope. No matter what I told him I knew it wouldn't get me out of the shit I was in. It was coming. The only questions were from who, when, where and how bad. I thought I could handle it.

The office was stuffy and hot. I turned on the air conditioner in my office, the fan by Renee's desk and opened the doors between the offices.

I made phone calls to a few roommates of Michael Lawson's from years before he had disappeared. No one knew anything. I even called two professors he had at Brown. None of them remembered him. He was a ghost. He treaded lightly everywhere he went. I couldn't imagine how he fit in with Benny, Paul, and the money owed. I decided Heather was reaching out for him in desperation.

Hope walked in the door when the clock read 10:49. 41

minutes early says something. He had a thin case. His canvases had come up with nothing. He needed anything he could get. He was desperate. He was anxious to see me.

"Hope?"

"Graves, good to see you"

"Come on in."

"Pretty good set up you got here."

"It keeps food off the table."

"Ha-ha. This is my partner, Ricky Stein."

Hope was lean, sharp and black. He came off as prepared and reserved. I got the impression he was expecting the other shoe to drop. He wore a light gray pinstriped suit befitting a lawyer. Rick Stein, on the other hand, was a kid the Spartans would've taken one look at and happily thrown into a bear cave. And for good reason too. He was improperly proportioned and sporting an outfit of varying shit-like shades. He came off as suspicious and arrogant; qualities embodied by many cops and irritating in every case.

"Good to meet you."

"Yeah, thanks."

"Okay"

Stein loved being a cop and that always pissed me off. I motioned for them to follow me into my office. I sat behind my desk and they sat down in the two chairs in front of my desk. Hope sat down first, saying, "Sorry we're early."

"Not a problem."

Stein butted in. His tone was hard to tolerate.

"We heard you had a robbery?"

"You heard right."

"There aren't a lot of robberies in Midtown East. Especially offices like this."

Stein scoffed. I didn't care. So I mocked his tone and gesture parroting, "Like this?"

Hope tried to reconcile the situation quickly. "Let's just get down to it and we can get out of your way."

"Fine"

"Alibi for two nights ago?"

"I met a friend for a drink uptown around five. I got some food from Leon's at about seven. Other than that I was home. Only corroboration I've got is that I made a phone call to my secretary later that night."

Stein chirped in, saying, "Where's your secretary, R.T.?"

"Not here, Ricky."

"What do you know about Paul Jensen?"

"Not much. I know he's dead. We met the other night for the first time."

"This would be the night before last?"

"Yeah he was at Leon's and then followed me home."

"Followed you to your place? What for?"

"He was there five minutes. He wanted to find someone."

"Who?"

"Heather Lawson. She's a client."

"Have you got a number and an address?"

"Yeah, I do... but you can look it up yourself."

"Oh really?"

"Confidential client information"

"What did Jensen want with Heather Lawson?"

"It was my impression that someone was putting the screws to him to find her."

Stein had to chime in with "Was that your impression?"

"That's what I fucking said, isn't it?"

Hope motioned for Stein to back off and he began questioning me. "He takes some getting used to. But throw us a break here."

"There's nothing to catch here, Hope. He didn't mention any names. He was distressed. He left between 7:30 and 8."

"Did he say where he was headed?"

"No, he stormed off."

"But not before you gave him your card?"

"...I gave him my card incase he needed help. You

really got so few leads that you're gonna spend your morning fucking with me?"

"Well…I got a few leads. His wallet's missing. He had bruising from catching a beating sometime before he died. So it may be a simple mugging gone bad, but his girlfriend is pretty sure it was something more sinister; says he knew a couple badass characters. But then again she's grieving with a year old baby girl and she hates the world. She's…distressed, to say the least. Me, I'm distressed because the two casings CSU found were right next to your card. And those casings and that card were the only things at the scene that we pulled any partial prints off of. So I got enough to fuck with you forever. But I don't want to do that. I want to extend to you the courtesy that you don't expect by coming to your office and being straight up with you. In turn, I want you to extend me the courtesy that I don't expect and explain to me what you did. Straight up."

"I thought he was trying to jump me."

"Jump you?"

"He startled me. It wasn't a fight but it might explain a bruise or two. But when he left my place he was very alive and very scared of someone that was not me."

"So to clarify, Jensen was waiting for you at a bar near your apartment, he followed you to your apartment, he startled you, you didn't get into a fight but you… wrestled, you gave him your card, your best wishes and you parted ways."

"He didn't follow me to my apartment. He was already there waiting…but other than that, it looks like you got the general idea."

"You coming clean with me, Graves?"

"Hey, I'm all for professional courtesy."

"See…I'm having a hard time believing that this guy chased you down, wrestled with you, harassed you about a client and then you just gave him your card."

"You believe what you want. But the facts are: I have

no motive and I didn't fucking do it."

On that note, I stood up. Hope and Stein followed suit. Hope re-buttoned his suit coat as he continued, "You're a detective, Graves. You were the last one to see him alive. He's looking for a client of yours. You two got in a tussle. He's found without a wallet. Your card is lying on the ground. And the gun you reported stolen two days ago matches up with the caliber of the murder weapon. Should I be looking at you?"

"Get serious. I'm too lazy to murder. And get over the departmental jones to put me away. You should be looking at Jensen's friends and family. People might push him to locate Heather Lawson and who would want him dead if he didn't. But to tell you the truth, I don't give a flying fuck what you do, because you can't pin this on me."

Stein spoke up.

"We don't put it past a disintegrating son of a bitch like you to stage a break in, hide your piece and then pop a kid... even if you barely knew him."

"You think I've got the energy for conspiracies too?"

Hope put his hand up, and said, "When the ballistics and the prints come back, I'm going to put you at the scene. Then, you're really going to have to straighten up.... Or I'm going to be back with bracelets and an arrest warrant. There's more going on here than you're letting on."

I was barely listening to Dante's intimidation efforts. I have no patience for such preposterous amounts of crap. I just continued to crack my neck and roll my eyes until there was a lull and I managed to say, "Thanks for stopping by, fellas."

They were at the outer door when I asked Hope one last question.

"Where were you before the 15th?"

"What?"

"Where you working before the 15th?"

"Internal Affairs..."

Hope slammed the door behind him. He'd aged. He used to shave his head and have a goatee. I never heard him speak. I only saw him behind a desk or in the back of a room. He was there, but he may as well not have been for all the attention I gave him. He was always in IAB. There are three types of people who work IAB: ambitious maggots, ambitious politicians and ambitious idealists. Whichever he was, he wasn't likely to like me.

Heather Lawson didn't pick up each of the four times I phoned. I was perturbed.

Pierce was next on my shit list. I desperately wanted to bitch at him. Instead, I ran down the list of everyone who popped up in my searches for Heather or Michael Lawson. The only person to pick up or give me the time of day was a woman Heather shared a lease with years earlier.

"Hello"

"Hi, Ms. Bernstein. My name's Graves. I'm a private detective. I was wondering if you could answer a few questions about...Heather Lawson."

"What kind of questions?"

"She was your roommate."

"Yes"

"You don't live together anymore, do you?"

"No"

"Do you know where she lives these days?"

"Probably with Sam or Elsa"

"Elsa and Sam are friends of hers or yours?"

"They're her friends."

"Do you have last names for Elsa and Sam?"

"Elsa, I have no idea. Sam's last name is Carlyle or something."

"Okay."

"Sam had a place in the village. I'm not sure where."

"Is Sam her boyfriend?"

"...Hah. No...Look, I'm just not...sure I should be talking to you."

"Why's that?"

"I'm just...not sure."

"It's fine. Actually, Heather hired me for my services the other day. She isn't picking up the number she gave me. I'm just looking for anyway to catch up with her."

"I'd be surprised if she paid a phone bill."

"She's ...nomadic. I take it."

"You could say that."

"Would you take down my number, and if you happen to--"

"She won't come see me."

"I think she may be desperate. Desperate times call for leaching off old friends."

"She won't come see me because I won't help her... but if you find her...tell her I hope she's okay."

"Why? Had she been not okay?"

"...Good bye."

"Oh, one last question."

"...Yes"

"Did you know Michael Lawson?"

"My god, is that who you're really looking for? Jesus. You tell Sam and Heather, that...after this many years it's ridiculous."

"Why do you say that?"

"I moved on years ago. Being involved with her was... destructive. I would really appreciate it, if you wouldn't call here again. Good bye."

Her disdain for Heather's lifestyle only made me more hesitant. The scales were heavily favoring the "quit while you're a few grand ahead" side. I went on investigating because I had been sucked far enough under that I would drown in the sand if I didn't proactively search for an out.

I looked through some of the papers I had on Michael Lawson's assorted residences. 'S. Carlson' paid the utilities for his loft sporadically. But then 'S. Carlson' started being billed at a place on Charles Street. I figured Michael and Carlson had roomed together for a bit. I was still looking up Carlson when my phone rang. I wedged the phone between my shoulder and ear.

"Graves Investigations"

"Mr. Graves?"

"This is he."

"It's Heather Lawson."

"Ms. Lawson, I've been trying to get a hold of you."

"You found Michael?"

"No. There have been some…developments that we need to discuss: namely your popularity."

"What do you mean?"

"Paul Jensen, Benny Chan, the police."

"What did you tell him?"

"Which him?"

"Benny"

"I didn't tell him much of anything because I don't know much."

"There's nothing to know. Benny has nothing to do with what I'm paying you to do."

"True, but when punks like Benny start showing up at my office and harassing me, it starts to have something to do with me, either personally or professionally. And with Jensen dead--"

"He's dead?"

"Yeah. He turned up in an alley this morning."

"Damn it, Paul. I never meant for anything like that to happen to him."

"While that seems plausible, I think you have a responsibility to go and tell--"

"I can't go anywhere."

"Yes you can. And you very much need to. The police are very unpleasant people, but you need to deal with them right now."

"I can't."

"This is not some trivial shit, Heather."

"Washington Square Park. There's a little place with benches… at the northeast end of the park. You show up there and I'll come to you."

"I don't want to see you. The police need--"

"I can't go to the police. I know this isn't part of your job, but maybe you can get them off my back. I just need some time to figure things out, to get Michael and… there are just some things I don't want to say on the phone. Please. I'm desperate for someone to help me."

"You have gotten yourself into a spectacular situation, haven't you?"

There was a pause and desperation loomed in her silence. I don't know what compelled me to agree. Either gross stupidity or some neglected sense of compassion took a hold and I mumbled into the phone, "Thirty Minutes."

"Thank you. Make sure you aren't followed."

She hung up. I cracked my neck. It was a bad idea to meet her. It made me squeamish. But I put my jacket on and locked the door behind me whilst praying my phone wasn't tapped.

Outside, there was a suspicious looking character leaning up against a street lamp. He got so excited upon spotting me that I laughed. He was obviously not a cop. But there was a conspicuous Crown Vic parked halfway down the block. It pulled out as I made a right.

I made my way towards the entrance for the 6. One of the cops got out of the car. I ducked into a coffee shop on the corner, waited for the cop to follow me in, asked rhetorically where the bathroom was, headed right for the door to the kitchen and the back exit. I hustled down the alley and around the corner. I took off my jacket and made it into the 51st station, wheezing. I prayed they wouldn't catch me on the platform or at the next stop. It wasn't a pretty escape, but it worked.

I got off at Astor Place and walked to the park, drenched in paranoia. I sat on a bench near the corner with my jacket across my lap. She arrived wearing a hooded sweatshirt and jeans, but still looking cold.

"Can you find Michael?"

"I don't know. With all this shit going on, it doesn't seem all that--"

"It is. It is the most important thing right now. If I can talk to... Michael, then I can work everything out. This can be fixed."

"You think he can fix this?"

"Yes. This whole situation. If he knew what was going on and what was at stake, he'd do the right thing. I know him and I know he would."

"I really don't think that he is going to be able to do much."

"He has money."

"That's not--"

"What do you want? More money? You can have it. If I find him, everything will be okay. It really will."

"He's a ghost. Most people that have moved, operated heavy machinery, gotten a parking ticket, had a phone, paid a utility bill, bought a plane ticket or lived within the guidelines of normative behavior for a man in his thirties can be found. He cannot. He is off the grid. Look, all the shit I've gathered goes nowhere. None of it is useful. You get me? Either he's dead or he doesn't want to be found, either way I'm not finding him without a lot of luck."

"He isn't dead."

"The point is we don't know anything."

"I know he isn't dead."

"What aren't you telling me? I mean I know there's a heap of shit you aren't letting me in on and usually I don't care because I don't really need to know. But at this point, I need to know what you know. Or else I will drown along side you. Catch my drift, sweetheart?"

"He must be reachable."

"How do you--"

"Because...someone talked with him a little while ago. I heard them on the phone and--"

"Who? If they called from your phone I can find the number on the phone bill and backtrack."

"No, you can't do that."

"Why not? Who are you afraid of?"

"Are you kidding? ...Everyone."

She was absolutely serious and I was fed up. I was beginning to understand why people would shy away from helping this crazy woman.

"C'mon. You need to go to the police."

"I knew you wouldn't help me. Why would you want to help me? Nobody cares. You don't care. You just want to get paid. Do your job and you'll get paid. Find Michael, how is that so hard for you to comprehend?"

"If you don't give me anything else to go on, I can not find Michael Lawson. He severed all connections. Unless you want me to call your father for you, I have no idea how to--"

"No. No. You cannot do that. You can't call him. He won't talk to you. He's-- Fuck him."

"That's what you said before, but I just don't have any other options. If you want him--"

"No, you cannot talk to Leo Lawson. Try everything else. Exhaust every other resource. There has to be a way. And if they come back, then we can work this all out."

"I have exhausted just about every resource. Between yours, Benny C's and everyone else's bullshit orbiting around me... something has to give. So give."

"I'm sorry if Benny C and the cops are bothering you, but believe me I have bigger problems than how irritated you are. You think your life is hard? You think you've got a tough job?"

"Don't get confused. Wading around in shit up to my neck is not in my job description."

"That's right. Your job is to find Michael. That's it."

"You aren't hearing me."

"I have to go."

"Wait a second."

"Stop. Stop. Look, I heard stories about you and I thought you could ignore the other shit here and just get done exactly what I needed from you. But if--If I was wrong than keep the retainer and forget about it."

"What stories?"

"Ha-ha. He'll kill you if you get involved."

"Benny C couldn't kill a smart cockroach."

"Ha-ha. Benny?"

"Then who?"

"You know who he works for."

"No, I don't. His old boss is doing a decade in Otisville."

"Not anymore."

"You're mistaken."

"Believe me. I wish he was still in jail."

"He couldn't have gotten out. Not this early."

She trounced off, only turning around to say, "If you really like pay days, find Michael, Graves. And call me."

My gut just told me that something was off. She blinked funny. Her mannerisms were shaky, but slow. Considering what I had done, it was beginning to look like crazy was infectious.

I was somewhere between downright pissed and perturbed as I went back to the office. Renee was lounging on the couch with her crutches propped against the wall.

"I thought I told you not to bother coming in."

"Who says I listen to you?"

I cracked my neck and didn't bother to retort. She recalibrated and started in again.

"I got bored at your apartment. I thought I'd come in and clean up a little bit; check the messages. What's bugging you?"

"Messages?"

"They're on your desk."

"I'm fine. How you feeling?"

"Better. The swelling is down. It doesn't hurt to walk on."

"Stick with the crutches."

I looked through the messages aimlessly. I couldn't

figure anyway to clear up anything. Heather had mystified a beautifully simple case. I didn't want to know what the fuck was going on. It never really paid to know what was going on.

But I had the feeling it could be my ass if I didn't figure out at least a little bit of what was going on. I got out my pad and glanced at Charlie Goldstein's information. I threw down the messages in frustration.

"Shit. Can you handle this?

"Yeah"

"I should go see that fucking guy Garcia told me about, Goldstein; works on Seventh. I'll see you at the apartment."

"No. Graves, I need to go home."

"What?"

"I need to do some things."

"Like what?"

"… Like get clothes and--"

"Take some of Mary's."

"No. Graves, I have--"

"Okay. Go back to my place. Hang around. As soon as I'm finished with this guy on Seventh Avenue then we'll deal with it together."

"No, it's easier if I just go back home."

I was almost out the door. I pulled back, sighed and plead with her.

"Wait for me. Please."

"All right."

"Thank you. Don't forget to lock up."

CHAPTER SEVEN

The building was on Seventh; right in the middle of Fashion Row. I knew that because I passed two guys selling fake leather pants out of the back of a beat up Lexus on the way in.

It was an average office building. I made my way to the front desk and the two security guards behind it.

"Looking for Charles Goldstein."

"Sign in. Identification?"

"ID? Yeah, sure."

"Seventeenth floor. There's a receptionist desk up there."

"Have a good one."

"You too"

The elevator doors opened to a chic waiting room. Almost everything was bright white, including the shag carpet but excluding the orange sofa. The receptionist had a head set on. She was flipping through a thick fashion magazine when I saddled up to the desk.

"Hello. How can I help you?"

"I'm looking for Mr. Goldstein."

"Do you have an appointment?"

"I don't, but if you could just tell him that I was

referred by Sam Garcia. And that I'm a detective."

"Can I see your badge?"

"I'm the private kind of detective."

I handed her one of my cards.

"I don't know if he'll see you...He's in the design--
Well, let me go and check."

"I appreciate it."

The girl hustled off through one set of glass doors and
down a hallway. Ten seconds later she emerged with a man
in tow. He had a measuring tape draped around his neck.
His shirtsleeves were rolled up. He was bald, barefoot and
barreling towards me.

"Yes?"

"Mr. Goldstein?"

"Yes. Look, if you're Sammy's muscle for MOMA
thing--"

"No. No. I'm a private detective and an old friend of
Sam's. He said you might be able to help me out."

"With what?"

"The Lawson's"

"Leo 'The Lion's' Lawson's?"

"That's not really what you call him, is it?"

"Why oh why dear boy do you want to know about the
boring old Lawson's?"

"From what I've seen and heard they aren't so boring."

"Oh I know much spicier families. Families with some
pizzazz..."

"I'm sure you do. I'm actually looking for some
information about the children, Michael and Heather."

"Well, I guess they would be the more interesting parts
of the family unit."

"Is there some place we can speak privately?"

"For you...   My office. We can avoid these
unscrupulous gossips that call themselves my employees.
... Michelle! Tell Marco that he better clean up the dress
and if he hasn't sewed it up by the time I'm finished with
this tall, dark stranger, I will have his balls skewered."

Goldstein was ferocious. I didn't want to get in his crosshairs. I hoped to be forgotten before I could be remembered. His office was filled with photographs, magazines, artwork, fabric swatches, clothes and a lot of unidentifiable stuff. There were no family pictures, just colossal shots of gaunt models in their gear. Charlie threw his feet up on his desk.

"What type of investigation are you conducting?"

"The complicated type"

"Are you typically engaged for simple matters?"

"Not typically. But I'm best at simple matters."

"I'm disappointed, Mr. Graves. Where's your sense of adventure? Your grand pursuit of justice?"

"Missing"

"No highly conscionable code of conduct?"

"Not really"

"No getting the bad guy?"

"I'm a private detective. I am the bad guy."

"Oh...very edgy. I like it. I like you. But the Lawson family--they are just plain boring ...these days."

"They weren't always boring?"

"No, not always. I shouldn't even speak this poorly of them, not after all that poor Leo's been through recently."

"His wife?"

"Yes, you heard."

"It was in the Times."

"Oh, I know. She wasn't a particularly warm person, but she did have some good qualities. A minor patron of the arts, one could say."

"Anything you could tell me about the kids; relationships, friends, enemies, issues--"

"Dirt. I'm not close with any of the nuclear family. ...But we do share some loquacious friends."

"Blabby friends are always good."

"They're my favorite kind. I don't know much about the children's lives before they started getting in trouble. That's when they became worthy of conversation. Mr. and

Mrs. Leo Lawson were the regular, old, boring blue blood sort. No cheating, no lies, real close...shoot me now, you know. Anyway the kids grew up blah blah blah. Michael was into the entire eastern lifestyle. Buddha. Samurais. Whatever. He tried to be an artist, but neither genetics nor chance serviced him well. I think he finally gave up and moved out of town about five years ago. Michael never stirred up anything too juicy. But Heather--"

"Wasn't the perfect princess she was supposed to be?"

"That depends on your definition of perfect. If perfect is a coke-loving, money grubbing slut who cares about nothing and nobody aside from drugs, sex, and Louis Vuitton then... she was perfect."

"Coke?"

"Most definitely. She got kicked out of every private school from Dalton on down. No boarding school would take her. She ended up anywhere with fast boys and girls and a luxurious variety of in vogue drugs. It was coke, then ecstasy, then pharmaceuticals, then--"

"I get the picture."

"When her parents had cocktail parties, she would be at one of the other parents' casas having coke and tail parties. And if they weren't doing that, they were maxing out daddy's Black Card buying bottles. It's a popular trend. But most snap out of it. She didn't. Every time I saw her in those days she had pupils the size of saucers."

"So you'd say she had a serious drug problem?"

"Well, it wasn't comical. I would say that since she was 16, blow has been the driving force in her upbringing. She did half a dozen stints in rehab; none of them took. She used to be a beauty too. I almost used her for one of my shows, a God's age ago, as a favor."

"She doesn't strike me as runway material."

"You've met her?"

"Briefly, twice. She's... difficult."

"I can imagine. Has she reconciled with her father?"

"That, I don't know."

"I'd heard that after her last rehab stint, Mommy dearest had had enough. Heather had pinched this beautiful diamond necklace; a six-figure gift from Daddy and Fred Leighton. So Lizzy told ole Leo that it was either his wife or his daughter. One was leaving. She wanted Heather completely cut off. I don't think Leo took it very well but he bowed to his wife and her wishes. Word was Leo took out restraining orders on the whole wild bunch of 'em."

"What about Michael?"

"Oh, Michael was a momma's boy. Mommy said he didn't have a sister. He said 'Okay. I don't have a sister'. That was how it went."

"Is that so?"

"And I asked if they had reconciled only because somebody once whispered in my ear that Leo made it clear to Heather that once Mommy took the big nap, Heather would be welcomed back with open arms."

"You don't say?"

"I know what you're thinking, but there couldn't have been any foul play. Mrs. Lawson had battled breast cancer for years. Cancer finally won out. "

"Yeah, cancer's a real winner. Can you rattle off any people Michael and Heather would've kept in contact with, or maybe...where Heather got her drugs?"

"These days they probably order them online. But as for friends ...I would assume that Carlson is floating around somewhere. The Jensen Boys. Carla Weiss. Ronnie Bass. Katie Ma-"

"Sam Carlson?"

"Yeah. Carlson was another blue blood, Michael's age, father died young, and the mother remarried poorly. Sam was at Brown--"

"While Michael was there?"

"Yes. We'll they'd have to have been there at the same time."

"Do you know what Michael's doing now?"

"No."

"So you don't know where he is?"

"Absolutely not. …But I heard Japan."

"Okay. Ha-ha. Thanks for your time."

"I think he liked Geisha girls."

"Some do."

"But not all… Mr. Graves?"

Things took an awkward and unintended turn.

"No, I didn't mean it like that. Everybody has their tastes."

"So what have you detected about my tastes, Mr. Graves?"

"I'm not here to profile you, Mr. Goldstein."

"All in good fun, Mr. Graves. Be a sport"

"Well… there's the fact you own a clothing design company."

"Bad stereotype to utilize in your investigation."

"That shirt…"

"Good taste."

"No wedding ring, pictures of the kids."

"Bachelor"

"You've had a pedicure."

"A well groomed bachelor"

"You didn't take as much as a glance at your secretary's ass or tits when she brought you to see me."

"I've already seen what there is to see."

"And Garcia told me you were gay before I came."

"Slander! It is shameful how vicious gossip can be. But alas the circumstantial evidence has mounted in your favor and my tastes have been detected."

"I didn't mean to offend you. Honestly, I apologize if I did because that wasn't my intention."

"Oh with you boys it's all about appearances. I enjoy a good bit of gossip because I get to make my assumptions about people with little unsubstantiated whispers. I let other people do the judging. What interests me so much about your profession, detecting, is that everything is based on appearances. You interpret what you see and detect what transpired."

"I rely on gossip as much as you do."

"Maybe, but you still make your deductions primarily from what you see; indisputable evidence. To detect is a naturally ocular occupation. I am not condemning you, Mr. Graves."

"You probably should be."

"Oh no. I just feel like you must live a life full of surprises."

"Surprises?"

"Yes. When the unexpected comes from the unexpected direction at the unexpected time from the unexpected person?"

"I'm familiar with the notion. But I know everyone is capable of everything. So I don't surprise easily."

"Then you must be a terrifically thorough detective. I've always found it quite difficult to see that which lies beyond the eyes. And what lies beyond the eyes is …truth."

"Poetic"

"Do you like that? I thought it was fitting. Make sure to quote me in future references. Charles P. Goldstein."

"It's a good thing to remember in my ocular endeavors for truth. Thanks again."

"Mr. Graves, I will tell you this: Heather Lawson's gay."

"Is she?"

"You're surprised!"

"No. …A bit, maybe. She's definitely got guys after her. Do you know any of her girlfriends?"

"Not off the top of my head. But her familiar relationships haven't flourished. I suspect her romances suffer from similar infertility."

"Thanks again. Have a good night, Mr. Goldstein."

"…Charlie."

"Charlie, my card. In case you ever need a scrappy

private investigator. I do runway stuff too."

"I'll keep that in mind, Mr. Graves. You know your way out."

I nodded and waved on my way out. Goldstein succeeded in making me feel like the considerable ass I am, though I'm sure I was far more offensive. I felt bad, but it was worth it for the few rumors he'd heard.

CHAPTER EIGHT

Renee was sitting with her back to my apartment door. I hauled her upright. The two of us made it to her town house before dark.

Renee seemed calm. She pushed her key into the keyhole and opened the door. Roberto was standing near the kitchen, his hair slimy at thirty feet. The sight of him made me yearn for a gun.

"Where've you been?"

"I stayed at Graves'."

"Thanks for babysitting, Graves. You can get out of my house now."

He was pissing me off before I heard him speak. Once words actually came out of his mouth, I knew things were going to escalate. It was only a question of how quickly and how Renee would react.

"Roberto, you fucking greased rat, why don't you--"

"This is husband and wife shit, Graves. It doesn't involve you. The door's right behind you."

"I'm about a millisecond away from--"

Renee put her hand on my chest. I shrugged and backed off. I wedged myself against the door waiting for the next opportune moment to speak. While attempting to keep my mouth shut, I occupied myself by cracking my neck.

"And don't bother calling or visiting or doing shit, Graves. You aren't welcome. And she's not working for you anymore. So you can fucking go or--"

"Are you really going to try to threaten me? You're as scary as dog shit."

Renee stood awkwardly between us. Finally, she bobbed her head and said quietly, "You should go."

"Then I'll go."

I conceded slowly, still hoping to be antagonized. I stood on the stoop. Renee stared at me. Roberto said nothing else, but slammed the door an inch in front of my face. I lingered. It was only a few seconds before I heard them arguing about me. Roberto yelled. The door opened. I was still on the steps. Renee looked at me. She was ready to check out. Roberto grabbed her arm and swung her around.

"Roberto, let go."

She struggled for a second. She gave me a telling look and I had all the approval I needed. I was happy. I pried his fingers off her arm in a not so delicate manner. I threw him back into the staircase and hit him with a quick combination of jabs, crosses and hooks in no particular order. He had no time to react. And it was by no means a fair fight. I liked it better that way.

With blood spattering the hardwood floors, I was ready to leave him without looking back. I only paused for Renee. She exhaled and shook her head.

"All I wanted to do was leave. And you couldn't even let me do that, you pathetic bully."

Roberto did look pathetic, but that wasn't enough to wipe the grin off my face.

"Renee, why don't you get some clothes and whatnot together?"

"Yeah. Will you stay with him?"

"I would love to."

She headed up the stairs. Roberto was spitting out some blood and making an effort to lean up against the wall.

"Don't you take one fucking piece of jewelry. Fucking slut."

I kicked him. Renee disappeared at the top of the stairs.

"Ya know, I'm happy, Roberto."

"I bet you are."

"I'm happy that she figured out she needed to leave on her own. I didn't even have to tell her about the girl you're banging every Tuesday and Thursday. But I will if you don't behave. And then she'll get more of your money."

Roberto spit a mouthful of blood on my shoes.

"Are you fucking kidding me?"

I kicked him until he was lying on his side, bleeding on his wooden floors. I then carefully used the back of his shirt to clean off my shoe.

"These are great fucking shoes."

Many minutes passed. Roberto managed to get himself back into a sitting position. I was sitting on the staircase when she started calling my name.

"Hey, Graves"

"Yeah"

"Can you help me with these bags…"

She had three bulging duffle bags near the top of the stairs.

"Looks like you got everything."

"I think so. Maybe I should double check."

"I think we should just go."

I hauled the bags downstairs and outside. Renee followed me, only hesitating to leave her ring on the banister.

Outside, I hailed a cab. Renee stood rigidly. I could tell she was fighting the urge to look back at the house.

"It'll be a fresh start. Right?"

"If you discount the grossly overweight baggage."

She gave a polite laugh, looking down as a cab pulled to

the curb.

"What happened to your shoes?"

"He spit on 'em."

"Oh God…Those were great shoes."

"It's just blood, maybe it'll come out."

"Of suede?"

I called Pierce on the ride home. He didn't pick up. I arrived at the apartment, after a twenty minute cab ride, to find it clean. Or at least straightened.

"You cleaned?"

"I straightened… a little. I was bored."

"I'm bored all the time. I never do anything that crazy."

"Well, I've got another crazy idea. If you go out and buy groceries, I'll cook you dinner… as thanks for the hospitality."

"I'm not much for hospitality, but I do like dinner."

Renee made a list as we went through cabinets and argued over what food needed to be thrown away. I was getting ready to leave when the phone rang. I picked up without thinking or checking the caller ID.

"Yeah… Hello."

"Rupert…"

The voice registered instantly. She took a deep breath after saying my name. I hung up before she could get another word in.

"Who was it?"

"Selling something I don't want. I'll be back in a bit."

The store was crowded but I made it out unscathed. My thoughts were scattered on my trek home. Mary and Renee were battling for superiority within my skull. One was waiting at home ready to make dinner. The other was in Europe making prank calls. That was what half of me thought. The other half thought that I was exploiting my fragile, beautiful, recently separated secretary at the apartment my wife bought and we shared until I pushed her to another continent. I was thinking myself nauseous.

Two blocks from the store, I noticed my amateur

shadow. He didn't react well when I tuned around to look in his direction. The kid nervously smoked a cigarette, staring blankly into a pharmacy window. I crossed the street. He followed. I rounded the next corner.

I quickened my pace, rounded another corner in a jog, and stopped to put down my groceries.

The kid took the corner in a full sprint and I took him by surprise.

"Where you running to?"

"What?"

"What do you want?"

"Hey, I don't know what you mean."

"Cut the shit, kid and spit it out. You commuting from uptown?"

"What?"

"If you're working for Benny or--"

"I don't work for them."

"Good for you. Neither do I."

I wasn't sure I should turn my back on him, but something about him seemed upstanding. Rather than engage in a ream of bullshit, I figured I might as well save my voice and walk away. He caught up again.

"I want to know who you're working for."

"I don't want to tell you."

"Well, do you mind telling me who killed Paul Jensen then?"

"I didn't. So I can't."

"You were the last one to see--"

"Try tailing Benny C, buddy."

"How do you know he did it?"

"I just said I didn't."

"Lisa said they found him with your card. And that he had just been to see you."

"He left my place in one piece. And I'm sorry, but I don't know what happened to him."

"He was just a normal dude."

He slowed his pace and halted midblock. Of all the

people I'd been dealing with, this kid struck me as the most worthy of help. I still didn't want to give him any, but I cracked my neck, cursed and turned back to say, "Normal dudes don't get involved with--"

"Paul wasn't involved. That was Heather and Sam."

"Do you know Rolando?"

"I've heard of him."

"And you've heard of him as someone not in jail."

"Yeah. Benny introduced Heather and Paul and all them. They thought he was—I don't know—cool or something. He was giving them good deals. ...I just don't get why he would kill Paul just like--"

"Leave it to the police, kid. They may be inept, but they are thorough. And they like solving cases. It gets them promotions."

"What about you?"

"I don't do murderers. I'm out of their league."

"You won't find out?"

"No. It makes no difference to me."

"Right..."

"Shit. I mean I am sorry about your friend. I just really can't help you."

"What if I paid you?"

" ...No. I don't want your money."

"Why would they kill Paul? They knew he didn't have the money. Nobody's seen either Sam or Heather in--"

I cut him off to substantiate what had become obvious.

"The money Heather ripped off Rolando?"

"Yeah"

"Was she doing a run for him?"

"I don't know. I just know he's out 450 thousand."

"He's out 450 thousand dollars. Why would he ever do that kind of business--"

"I don't know, man. I don't know what the fuck is going on. And I need to know. So you'll help me?"

"No."

I didn't give this one a card. I didn't even get the guy's

name. He lit up another cigarette. I continued on. The kid walked the other way.

Renee was halfway through a bottle of wine when I got home.

"I hope you don't mind. I opened some wine. Oh and you got a note from your neighbors. I didn't open it."

"Thank you. I can see that."

"They said to stop by when it was convenient."

I almost opened the note. But I came to my senses and threw it into the garbage.

"You aren't even going to read it? It could be heartfelt."

"Ha-ha. It's not. I've read it a thousand times. They leave one for me every couple of days. They always say please come by when it's convenient."

"I told them you would."

"When I regain my mental fortitude."

We were in close quarters moving around the kitchen cooking dinner. I figured that she seemed in fairly decent spirits and limbered by the wine. So I decided to get the embarrassment over with.

"I was thinking on the walk home--"

"What an achievement. Do you want a gold star or a medal, maybe a cash prize--"

"Both, but seriously I was thinking you're a soon to be divorcee--"

"As of a couple of hours ago"

"And so am I."

"...You are?"

There was actually sincere astonishment in her tone and the matching expression.

"I thought that was pretty apparent."

"No, I just thought... You know, that since you haven't really talked to her and--"

"I had Wilson draw up divorce papers months ago."

"So you're legally--"

"Well, she isn't exactly easy to locate."

"Right…"

"Anyway, I was thinking that tomorrow we could celebrate; turn over a new leaf together. Go somewhere."

Renee was fully unprepared for my advance. Her inebriation revealed her astonishment.

"On like a trip?"

"I was thinking more like dinner."

"Oh... Okay. Yeah, sure."

There was an awkward silence again as I felt the need to clarify the dinner as a date.

"I meant dinner as a date."

"Oh… Right. Graves, I just think… that if we--"

"It's fine. It is not a big deal."

"No. No. I just-- You know I don't think I've ever seen you this nervous before."

"I'm not nervous. It was just an idea, Renee. I get them every so often."

"I kind of like this side of you. Reeling and vulnerable."

"Forget it."

"You didn't give me time to answer. Aren't you curious as to what it would be?"

I took a moment, smirking nervously.

"Okay. So what's the answer?"

"I don't know. I could go either way."

"I rescind the--"

"Oh c'mon. Ask me again. Legitimately."

"Ask you again?"

"Yes. I want it nice and legitimate and heartfelt."

"Are you… talking to me?"

"C'mon…"

"Will you go out and have a lot of drinks and a small portioned fish dinner with me tomorrow night?"

"Yes. But I pick the restaurant."

"Okay"

"Okay"

I was proud of myself. But that didn't last long.

CHAPTER NINE

I dreamed well that night. It's no mystery why. I stopped by the guest room on my way down the hall the next morning. I tapped the door, which was slightly ajar, to get a better view into the room. Renee was sitting at the kitchen counter watching me tap the door to peek at her empty bed. She startled me.

"Good Morning!"

"Jesus. You scared the shit out of me."

I rubbed my neck, praying a reasonable response would come to me.

"…You made coffee?"

"I figured I had to start sometime."

"I knew I was going to like this arrangement."

"What?"

"Nothing… What do we do on your first emancipated day in New York?"

"I'm not sure… You don't have any work to do? Lawson case wise?"

"Not on Saturday, I don't. Any ideas?"

"No. You?"

"Not really."

"What do you usually do on Saturdays?"

"I don't know."

"Ha-ha. C'mon."

"I do crap. I don't know. I sleep late; later than this usually. I go have breakfast. I do nothing. I eat lunch, do nothing, eat dinner, do nothing and go to bed."

"When do you do all the betting and the drinking?'

"Before breakfast. I take it you don't have any pressing matters to attend to either?"

"I…can't really think of any pressing matters I need to attend to. I'm homeless, husbandless, pretty much hobby-less and money-less too. I can't work because you don't want to work. I like tennis and shopping. Do you like tennis or shopping?"

"No. I don't like either of those things."

"Then I got nothing. I do have a date tonight so get me back here before eight."

"Okay. Why don't we just go get some breakfast for now?"

"Okay."

"That won't take more than ten hours."

"I think it's more like brunch now."

"Let's not call it that, though. Let's leave brunch to women in scarves at the Boat House."

We ate at a diner on First. My wife always used to complain about how rundown the diner was. Renee thought it had a charming old fifties feel. We walked around aimlessly after we ate, ending up near Gramercy Park.

"You know, I got mugged just over there a couple years ago?"

"What? When was this?"

"I know it's shocking. Few years ago. Little skater kid took me."

"Somehow I can imagine that."

"Ah… It was the day after this A.D.A., my captain and I.A.B. cornered me in a conference room. I thought I was getting pulled off my detail and getting moved to a new precinct or getting a commendation or something. I showed up unwittingly. I had a badge, a service weapon and... an identity when I went in. I left with nothing. I was eleven weeks short of twenty years. The circumstances around my expulsion made it so most of the guys on the job severed all connections. I was never popular. But after it was all over, Pierce was the only cop speaking to me. A lot of guys have a serious identity crisis when they retire, get fired, whatever. The toughest guys I knew back in the day would be wrecks, sobbing in the alley at their retirement parties. That didn't happen with me. I didn't have a party or a friendly parting. I just drank myself into another plane of existence. And, during my recovery from one of the worst hangovers mankind has ever known, I got fucking robbed. ...Just over there"

"I'm sorry"

"Oh it wasn't that traumatic."

"Ironic"

"I guess."

"You got robbed by a... punk the day after you stopped being a cop. There's definitely some irony there."

"There's some embarrassment there...is what there is."

"Is that when you started the firm with Booker and Perry?"

"They had started it already. I came in afterwards. It was hard for me to get licensed, but it ended up happening. They gave me a good piece of the action and then you know the rest."

"They retired and you inherited the kingdom."

"Yup, my magnificent kingdom. A matchstick house. Sucker born every second."

I started thinking about how my shop was actually just about all I had. I certainly didn't like having it. But it was mine. After a few moments I chimed in, "Maybe I should do some detecting this afternoon."

"What are you going to do?"

"Benny C's parents own a Chinese restaurant in

Spanish Harlem."

"Let's go."

"You want to come?"

"What are we looking for?"

"We are looking for a Rolando Pequeno"

"What is a Rolando Pequeno?"

"It's a kind of asshole."

We walked to the Lexington and caught the 6 train. 'Chena Pan' had a small red awning a block from the subway. We stood across the street staring disparagingly through sunglasses at the restaurant with the faded red awning.

"Are we going in?"

"I wish I wasn't. I don't care, and I shouldn't... care or go in."

I was on my way in before I finished my sentence. I huffed, unhappy with the predicament and pining for an easy way out. Inside, I argued with Benny C's mother and left a note for Benny on the back of a menu. It read:

Benny, She can't be found. I quit. Don't come looking for me or the money you paid me. That's mine. Sincerely, Graves

Renee was sitting on the fire hydrant with her sunglasses on.

"She looked hostile."

"I'm not sure if his mother couldn't understand me or didn't bother to try."

"Probably the latter"

We went back to the apartment. I picked her up from the guest room around 7 and we were at the restaurant a half hour later. It was a crowded "wine" bar that she knew about but never got the chance to frequent. I told her that I thought the waiter might cry if I ordered Jack Daniels instead of wine. She laughed and said he looked like a crier. So things were going well. Then it went viciously silent and I feared an unhappy ending. Luckily, we drank more during the silence. And eventually, the booze took effect. She started regaling me with stories from her youth.

"You were in a band?"

"Why is that so hard to believe?"

"I don't know."

"Because I'm a girl?"

"No. Well maybe. What kind of band was it?"

"A normal bad rock band"

"Spiked hair, cut up jeans, I hate mommy, daddy and commercialism kind of band?"

"No"

"All girls in the band?"

"No. Two girls and three guys."

"Did you sing?"

"Why?"

"I've heard you sing."

"I've... won... ribbons for singing."

"So you were the front woman?"

"Something along those lines."

"I would've liked to have seen that."

"It was the 80's. I burned all the evidence. Now, you?"

"I'm an open book."

"That's not fair."

"What could you possibly not know about me after all this time?"

"You talk, but you don't talk about much. Like your past."

"There's a reason for that. And the past ain't ever the past. It's just obscured by the present."

"Okay so un-obscure something I'd want to know."

"I don't think you want to know that much. That's the point."

"C'mon. No 'On the job stories' either. I'm tired of police procedurals."

"I'm not going to come up with anything. My memory..."

"You're a bad sport. That's a terrible cop-out."

A familiar voice emerged from behind my ear.

"Graves! I hope you aren't wasting all my money on the escort."

Benny C stood beside our table. He had two thugs with him standing by the Maitre d's desk. His nose was obviously in bad shape. His face was still a swollen and accessorized with a white splint. The menu with my note was crumpled up in his hand.

"Please leave. People are trying to eat."

"What the fuck is this?"

He placed the menu on top of my food. I tossed it to the floor.

"That is a resignation, moron. See, I told you, Renee, four sentences was way too much for him to process."

"You can't fucking quit."

"I can and I did. I didn't guarantee I'd find her."

"I just said you can't fucking quit."

"I don't give a shit what you said, Benny. You need to get the fuck out of here now."

"Look, Graves. You are going to fucking tell us where she is. You are. One way--"

"You're making everybody lose their appetite."

"Listen--"

"I'm done with all this Lawson bullshit. I'm not doing any more work for her. I have no horse in this race. So seriously, go away."

"I'm not fucking around here, man. You had better bring her to us."

"Okay. Is it that you don't understand English or--"

"You really want to see what's going to happen if you fuck with us, Graves."

"Benny, if you don't get out of this restaurant in the next five fucking seconds, you're going to see something happen. And I am not kidding."

"This bitch--"

My chair flew back as I stood up. Renee threw her hand on top of mine. She ushered me to sit back down.

"Why don't you two stop acting like children? This is

embarrassing. Benny if would like to take a seat, you're welcome to."

"Nah, I don't want to sit down."

"Fine, then as Mr. Graves said, he will be unable to continue on in your investigation. The retainer you left covers his expenses and services rendered. It's over. On behalf of Mr. Graves, I apologize for the unsatisfactory results. We hope you find who you're looking for, but we've exhausted the resources at our disposal. If you call the office Monday morning, I would be more than happy to refer investigators who may have better luck with your case."

"Are you his secretary or his boss?"

"Both."

"...Alright. I warn you. If Heather Lawson don't show up soon, everybody's gonna pay. Right down the line."

Benny backed away. He and his two thugs departed. I tracked him through the restaurant and outside.

"Did you do that to his face?"

"No, he was born that ugly. I just accentuated one of his worse features."

"I don't think it was wise to piss him off like that."

I hesitated as Benny disappeared into the night.

"Guys like Benny C don't have much decency in 'em. He's a hoodlum; a wannabe gangster. Guys like him have IQ's south of a Popsicle stick. They only get the upper hand, if you give it to 'em. And they can only whip you with the slack you give 'em."

"I get the picture... but idiots and gangsters are still dangerous when they're pissed off. And armed."

"Trust me on this, Renee. This is nothing I can't handle."

"Well, I hope you're right, but I just don't trust you."

I wasn't taking it serious. But she was.

On the way home, I foresaw a gloomy end to the evening and her eventual departure from the apartment. So I made a serious effort.

"When I was about 10 my sister opened a lemonade stand at the end of the driveway."

"What?"

"She had the lemonade stand at the end of the driveway for a whole week during the summer. And for the first five days she got no business. She sold maybe five glasses and those were all to one neighbor. She was charging something like 25 cents a glass. High-end lemonade. My poor sister was such a bad businesswoman. She cried every night. So I told everybody in the neighborhood that if they each bought--I think I said ten glasses each, that I would give them each a signed Mickey Mantle rookie card. ...Then I went around to the girls who were my sister's age and told them I would buy them each a set of roller skates or a Beatles 45 if they bought ten glasses of lemonade from my sister."

"You didn't."

"I went to every other hot spot around the neighborhood. Telling everyone they would get signed Mickey Mantle memorabilia or Beatles' records or whatever I could come up with. Soon enough her business was booming, and I wasn't safe anywhere."

"Ha-ha. How'd you get away with it?"

"I didn't get away with shit. I got beat-the-fuck-up. They couldn't get their money back from Annie."

"Were you really hurt?"

"Yeah. My mom told me I'd live and it was nothing, but I had my doubts and cracked ribs. She called me Mickey for years after that."

"Really?"

"Mickey Mantle was my hook. Everybody knew I liked the Orioles and Frank Robinson. So I guess in their childish wisdom, it seemed plausible I'd be willing to part with the Mick. And I couldn't stand Mickey. But he'd just retired and the kids were nostalgic. ...That was my Dad's favorite story. He wasn't even in town when it happened, but he would tell that stupid story every time he went anywhere. You remember the time Rupert convinced the entire neighborhood Mickey Mantle would come over and give 'em hitting lessons. So for a long time I was known as Mickey in some circles. I hated it when they called me Rupert. Thomas wasn't much better. But I hated it most when they started calling me Mickey."

"You had 'em all fooled."

"Very briefly. So you got the story out of me. Is that sufficient or was it a cop out?"

"No, I liked that story."

She was still chuckling when we walked into the apartment.

"These shoes are killing me."

"Here let me help you."

Beautiful didn't begin to cover what Renee was. She was outrageously flawless in form and being. It sounds contrived, but she was so stunning. As soon as that thought had come and gone, it was replaced with another nearly as profound thought. Renee was too good for me. I truly and utterly did not deserve her. I knew Roberto didn't deserve her from the get-go. I deluded myself into thinking that I might be worthy. But as I stood over her in awe, a sudden feeling of insufficiency ran through my body. I craned my neck to watch her struggle with her shoes.

"What?"

"Nothing"

"What's that look?"

"No look"

She followed me into the kitchen. I watched her take off her earrings. I poured a glass of water for her.

"Here ya go"

"Thank you."

I was drunk enough to make my move at that point. The necessary lull in conversation had arrived. I helped her put down her glass, encroached and then she asked, "Did Mary call you 'Graves'?"

"Mary?"

"Yeah"

"No. Why would you? ...No"

"So she called you Rupert."

"Oh...um, yeah when she wanted my attention... Yeah, she called me Rupert."

"And you hate that?"

"Yeah. Most of the time."

"I wasn't trying to make you uncomfortable. I just wanted to know what she called you. And it's kind of weird and impersonal to always call you-- "

"She doesn't call me anything anymore, Renee."

"Does it make you uncomfortable to talk about her?"

"No, I would just rather not--"

"You're not over her?"

"Maybe not. Are you over Roberto?"

"Probably not. I think I'll call you Mickey from now on. We'll test it out. Goodnight, Mickey."

"Goodnight, Renee."

She rounded the corner and stepped out of sight. I exhaled a long breath. I couldn't help but grin. Another thought entered my head. I thought that even if I didn't deserve her, and never had her, I could still be around her. And being around her might just be good enough. Nonetheless, I reached over to the other side of the counter for a glass of consolation. I remember thinking what an awful, dumb drunk I was, reaching for the bottle. Renee's hand grabbed my wrist.

"I was joking before. I mean lying. I trust you."

"Okay"

"Because, you know, at dinner I said I didn't. But I was lying, and I trust you. I feel safe around you. I've always trusted you."

"Good. That makes--"

"Sometimes...I just worry. I know you're joking but some don't. I know you're whistling in the dark. And I know you've seen shitty things and dealt with shitty people. And I know you don't want to take the world too seriously, but these are dangerous people--"

"Especially women who had too much wine at dinner."

"Don't do that, Graves. Don't write me off like that."

"No. I didn't—I don't mean to do that. I don't have a problem saving my own skin. I've done it plenty of times. And... Look I try to be, for all intents and purposes, a callous ass. I don't know why, but I do. It wears thin ...especially when I spend too much time around beautiful women who figure out some of it's an act. I do care sometimes... for the select."

She towed me under right then and there. All it took was a kiss. It never takes much more.

CHAPTER TEN

Renee came into the bedroom with a cup of coffee. The situation had me very excited.

"You got me a coffee."

"Don't get used to it."

"I could."

She handed me the coffee and followed with a timid kiss.

"I think I'll go see Pierce today. Talk about the Benny thing."

"I think that's smart. That way it all be over with and you'll have nothing to complain about."

"Complain? Please. ...You just made me realize I'm going to have to take the fucking subway, the ferry and then walk. ...Fucking Staten Island."

The subway wasn't fun, neither was the ferry or the walk. I felt like fucking Columbus when I finally got to Pierce's house. The house was just small enough to irritably house a big family. He had 3 girls, not including his wife. Margie was most certainly a woman, and a handful. I used to pity the guy. I'd give him shit all day at work, and then he'd go home and take more shit. But he loved them so he put up with them. I'm not sure why he put up with me. Pierce was mowing the lawn when I walked up sweating.

"You take the ferry out?"

"Yes"

"And then walked?

"Yes and now I'm fucking sweaty. And I need a drink."

"You're sweaty? You need a drink? Look at me. I've been out here all day. And I didn't get any sleep last night. Diane came in last night two hours after her curfew. She-"

"Bitch. Bitch. Bitch."

"Oh. I suppose the shit on your plate is more interesting."

"I had an interesting night."

"You watch cartoons and pass out around eight with your thumb in your ass?"

"I slept with Renee."

"Oh sure you did."

"I'm beginning to regret it."

"Sure"

"I am."

"You didn't sleep with her."

"I did."

"No. She's too good-looking and ten years younger. And the world isn't that cruel."

"It is."

"Shut the fuck up. You've been wife-less for what... two years. You've bitched about how you dote over this girl's every move and now-- and now you sleep with her. I swore to myself I wouldn't live in a world where you sleep with your secretary. I swore I wouldn't. I'm going to have to kill myself now. You're going to have to take care of my family."

"Yeah, okay. If you could actually help me right now, I would appreciate that. I mean, we--she was drunk. And this morning she got me a coffee. And I don't want her to go, but how can I ask her to stay. Ya know?"

"Are you fucking kidding me? No. I don't fucking

know."

"Well, how about helping me out here?"

The screen door swung open as Pierce and I sat on the stoop. It was Margie. She was not happy to see me.

"Graves, I love you, but why the fuck are you at my house?"

"I came to talk to your husband."

"You're not allowed to."

Pierce asked, "Why not?" more inquisitively than indignantly.

"Because you know good and well that we have to go to the barbeque in fifteen minutes, and you haven't finished the lawn or dressed or showered."

"All right"

"It's not all right. And Graves, you cannot hold him up. You know how slow he is. And—And you two are not allowed to bullshit right now. Is that clear?"

We nodded and said, "Yes, Margie" in unison. She came up and kissed me on the head.

"I'm happy to hear you got laid."

Margie let the door slam behind her.

"You didn't really come all the way out here to gloat about sleeping with Renee, did you?"

"Not entirely. I need you play mediator with Hope. Benny C followed me to a restaurant last night. I told him to fuck off and it didn't end pleasant. Renee made the point it was a bad move. She's right and now that I know Rolando's holding some cards--"

"Rolando? You think he's running shit from what... Clinton."

"He was at Otisville. And apparently he's out, and in good health."

"Aw fuck. How'd I miss that? He rolled on someone. Must've. Maybe Summers finally."

"I don't know if even he's dumb enough to roll on his evil uncle."

"Have you seen him?"

"No, the Lawson girl and this kid both told me he was out."

"He must have rolled on Summers. We sent him upstate with god knows how many priors, the gun charge and Rockefeller weight. That's eight federal years no matter who his lawyer is."

"I just don't see that. Pissing all over his mother's brother, the man who raised him, even the prince of punks isn't rolling on his own blood like that."

"Rolando's mother's dead. She died right after the indictment."

"Did she?"

"She had a stroke or something. If she's dead, he's got fewer issues with rolling on Summers."

"If he's out and Summers isn't in then it's an ongoing investigation. DEA wouldn't tell you or me or anyone anything even if they did."

"Nor should they. Let them do the fucking job. It doesn't concern you. If he's out, he's out. DEA knows what's up better than you do, at least. I've got to go. I'll call Hope tomorrow morning and the three of us will have a sit down and work this out."

"He's going to try to push this murder wrap on me."

"Yeah. Well, you didn't kill him, did you?"

"No"

"Okay. So a murder wrap won't stick. Relax, you bitch."

"Tell him not to bring his fucking partner. That brat shows up and I may kill him."

"Yeah. Yeah."

Pierce was turning to leave when I said, "I have this feeling in the pit of my stomach like I'm fucked."

"What are you reluctant to save your own skin?"

"I still like my skin. It covers my body. I just got the feeling that maybe I should find out what's actually going on this time."

"That would be a change, but let's leave this to more

gifted professionals. I'll drop you off at the station on the way to this thing."

I struggled to get out Pierce's SUV as I was far too big too sit in the back with three adolescent girls. Margie waved me off with a bowl of fruit salad in her lap.

I took the ferry and the subway to return home. Renee was reading a magazine on the couch in the apartment.

"Hey. How'd it go?"

"He's going to arrange a meeting with Hope, play mediator."

"Good."

We sat silently apart for the better part of the day. We read, sat around and did nothing. Conversations died easily. I think she may have slept with me again that night solely for a break from the silence. The next day she was getting dressed in the guest room as I woke up.

"I'm going to go in early."

"Okay…you all right?"

"Yeah. I'm fine. I just feel like being productive. When are you going to come in?"

"As soon as I clean up and eat."

"Okay. Bye."

She gave me an unexpected kiss goodbye. She turned to walk out.

"You're limping. Take your crutches. …Please."

I heard the crutches clatter as she closed the door to the apartment behind her.

I fumbled around in my boxers for a while. Before I could make coffee, there was a rapping at the door. I was slow to get the door. A clean-cut stiff stood on the landing. He was six two, well built, with blonde hair, glasses, a pricey suit and contempt chiseled in his cheekbones.

"Would you mind coming down stairs?"

"Mind telling me who you are? Or what for?"

"I'm double parked."

"Pal, I'm far too grumpy to do something I don't have

to."

"Black Mercedes. We'll be outside."

After considering my new personal decree to avoid giving in to curiosity and inquiries into suspicious characters, I grabbed my keys, locked the door and headed downstairs. The Mercedes was double-parked.

"Aren't you going to put on any pants?"

"Why? Who you got in there? ...No answer. At this point on a Monday morning if it isn't the Pope or the Queen of England, I'm going in pants-less. The door, James."

He opened the back door to the car. I saw his glistening baldhead. I made sure to sit far enough away from the old sack of bones. He had pupils like a dehydrated junkie. It wasn't too hard to imagine him being feared, especially by his daughter.

"Go ahead, Gregory. Mr. Graves, my name is--"

"I know who you are, Mr. Lawson."

"We haven't met before, have we?"

"No"

"Not at a police benefit or--"

"I never really got to be a part of any of the police benefits."

"No. Well, I don't want to be here any more than you do. I'll get to the point."

"Please do."

"It has come to my attention that a certain someone retained your services for some kind of wild goose chase... to find my son."

"Mr. Lawson, I don't make it a habit to discuss my clients or my cases. They're private investigations."

"That's ethical of you. I'm only here to save you time and agony."

"How's that?"

"My son isn't missing."

"I'm happy to hear that."

His gentle façade dissipated and an edge crept into his

tone.

"Let's not fuck about. I know Heather hired you. And I know she hired you to find Michael."

"I don't know what--"

"He's in Japan."

"Japan?"

"Yes. Michael was always fascinated by Asian cultures."

"Was he?"

"I send him money every month. He works and travels."

"Well… Thanks for the rundown and the update, Mr. Lawson. But if you could just let me out--"

"Don't try my patience, Mr. Graves."

"I wouldn't dream of it."

"Give it up. Give up the case."

"Maybe if you give me a phone number and address for his place in Tokyo then we can work something out."

"I don't believe I mentioned anything about Tokyo. And I don't believe I'm prepared to compromise my son's privacy quite yet."

"Why does he need to be anonymous?"

"Michael cherishes his privacy… as do many, including myself."

"Couldn't get enough privacy in the city, eh?"

"No"

"Well if you're not going to tell me where he is or how to contact him specifically, I don't see how you're helping me. And I don't see the case ending. Heather will keep hiring--"

"There's nothing to investigate. So drop the investigation."

"That's not up to me."

"My daughter is a stubborn and unstable person. I have no intention of seeing her or attempting to dissuade her. I would prefer that you quit."

"My job has a pretty short lifespan anyways."

"In the last six years I've had to see an end to four

private investigations into my son. You'll either quit now or you'll be made to quit."

"I don't like ultimatums."

"You are a businessman, Mr. Graves, are you not?"

"A poor businessman, yes."

"But a businessman, nonetheless. So if I were to offer you somewhere in the vicinity of ten thousand dollars, would you give up the case?"

"I don't make it a habit--"

"Twenty thousand then. I don't care about your habits. And I will have to request all information you've gathered during your investigation. Everything"

I cracked my neck.

"I'd like to tell you to fuck off, but you're just too sweet of a negotiator."

"It's a deal?"

"Sure. It's a deal."

"Good. Bring us back to Mr. Graves' apartment."

"Would you like to come down to the office to pick everything up?"

"For twenty thousand dollars, I think you can have it couriered over to my office. My card."

He removed his wallet and took out a card. Lawson then took out his checkbook. With one hand he reached for his pen while he secured the check on the center bench of the back seat. He wrote quickly but signed delicately. The sound of the tear was like a symphony.

"You sure it won't bounce?"

"Yes."

"I was ah... I'll have my secretary take care of everything."

"Goodbye, Mr. Graves. I expect this will be the last time we see each other. Excuse me for interrupting your morning."

"Right. Thanks for the pay off."

The check even smelled good. Unlocking the door to my apartment, I noticed another note under the door. I ripped it open. It read:

> Please stop by and see us.
> Thank You,
> Norman and Claudia

I put it with the others.

CHAPTER ELEVEN

Renee was hobbling between file cabinets without her crutches. The office was beginning to resemble its pre-robbery state.

"Use your crutches."

"They get in the way."

"That's what they're supposed to do: Get in the way of you hurting yourself worse."

"Fine. On a happier note, Boss, business has sky rocketed. You have a 2 o'clock, 3 o'clock and 4 o'clock. And that Oil and Gas lawyer, Archer, wants you to come in at the end of the week, and Lew Adams called to say he would really like to talk to you about doing another round of interviews, but at the home office in Houston."

"No shit?"

"All called this morning. Appointment wise... Mr. Gonetti thinks his wife may be cheating on him. That's your 3 o'clock. Mr. Winston would like to have you follow his son. That's your 2 o'clock. And Mrs. Dobbs has the sneaking suspicion that her husband is going on too many 'business trips'. That's the 4 o'clock."

"Eh things are looking up, baby. Way fucking up."

I sat down at my desk. I withdrew Lawson's check

from my coat pocket. I pushed back the piles of shit on my desk. A few files and papers fell off. Once I had made a suitable clearing, I placed the crisp green check in the middle. I mumbled, "Things are looking good" to myself. After I repeated that a few times, the smile wore off my face. I started thinking, and repeating something else. "And things are never what they seem." All I could do was stare at the check made out to R.T. Graves for the sum of 20,000 dollars and 00/100 cents.

"Hey Renee, call Hal for me and put it through."

"Why? Are you pawning off the work?"

"No but I may have Hal do some of the dirty work."

"You haven't even been hired yet."

"Would you please call Hal?"

"I don't see why. Work is work. Money is Money."

"Thank you, Secretary."

"You should listen to your secretary more often."

"I'm always listening to her. That's the problem."

"You do have more to lose in offending me now."

"I immediately regret what I said. I love the sound of your voice. So will you read the number to me?"

Hal was at home and agreed to come in right away. I farmed work out to him when I needed someone dependable and punctual.

I put together everything I had on Michael and Heather Lawson. It all fit neatly into one manila envelope. I wrote 'Attention: Leo Lawson' on the cover.

"I'm going to get a coffee. Want anything, Mickey?"

"Are you going to get one of those girly coffees?"

"Yes, I'm getting a girly coffee."

"Oh okay"

"What do you want?"

"Nothing on the girly coffee front, but before you go, write up a receipt for services rendered, for Leo Lawson, deposit this check and then take this folder, photocopy everything inside first and then get it to the address on this business card."

"Jesus. Twenty thousand. When did you run into Leo Lawson?"

"This morning, right after you left. He paid me to quit looking for Michael Lawson, which is pretty convenient since we came to the general conclusion it was in our best interests to take that very course of action."

"You're cool with taking a pay-off like that?"

"Very cool. Money is money."

"Very funny"

"A wise woman once told me that."

"While I'm glad you listen to wise women, cashing this check does put you in a precarious and unethical situation."

"Oh don't do that. Don't ruin this for me. I'll buy you a damn air conditioner."

"I'm just saying--"

"Fine. Say, 'Rip it up.' And I'll do it."

I was actually holding the check out in front of her, making a small tear in the top of the check. She grabbed it from my hand.

"Thank you."

"I hope you don't regret it."

"No, wait. Shit. You're a cripple. Stay. I'll do the errands."

"I'll do them. I'm fine. And you have to wait for Hal."

"Take your crutches."

"You think you're the boss of me, Mickey?"

"You realize I really don't like the Mickey thing, right?"

"Oh yes"

Renee left. Hal arrived twenty minutes later. Renee was still out.

"Hal"

"Yeah. What? Are you locking your doors now?"

"Had a break in the other day."

"That's no good. They take anything?"

"My gun"

"That's trouble."

"Yeah. I've got to fucking buy a new gun and re do all my permit shit. Anyway, I've got appointments at 2, 3 and 4. All shadowing jobs as far as I can tell, some clicks with the camera, a little paper pushing and phone calls maybe."

"Do you want me to handle one of 'em?"

"Two of 'em, if you're up for it."

"Two. My lucky day has finally come in."

"How long have you been waiting for it?"

"A couple decades."

"60/40 split. You get the lion's share and you handle everything on the two cases."

"You love negotiating, right? How bout we make my 60 into 70."

"65. Two cases, Hal. You're writing the reports."

"Okay. You want me around this afternoon?"

"If you don't mind"

"I've got nothing better to do. One of the few perks of my painful retirement. What have you got going on that you can't handle these cases yourself?"

"I'm just wrapping up this fucking pretzel case. I'm trying to crawl to safety."

"Been on it for a while?"

"A week. But it's taking a hold of me."

"Getting curious?"

"I'm trying not to."

"Lonnie Murphy always used to say--"

"Curiosity makes quicksand."

"Curiosity makes quicksand. That's right."

"Lonnie said it better though, but all his preaching didn't end up helping him."

"That's true. At least he went out swinging."

"But he went out."

"Got any coffee?"

"Only if you make it."

Hal wrestled with the coffee machine while we reminisced about Lonnie Murphy. Then the kid who had been tailing me, Paul Jensen's nameless friend, came through the door. He looked unkempt and emotionally battered.

"You said come back next week and now it is next week."

"I also said I don't work on murder cases. I'm not fucking Colombo, kid. And I don't have a badge."

"I brought some money."

The kid removed a few crumpled twenties and tens from his pocket. It was no more than a hundred bucks. It wasn't much of an incentive. It wasn't nearly enough to get me to jump back into the Lawson case, after I had just started to crawl my way out.

"It's not a lot. I mean you probably get more usually, but I-- I figured maybe you were like already working on the case, kind of, and it's all--all I could come up with. Lisa doesn't want me to hire you. Is it enough?"

"No. It isn't enough."

"Oh"

"Who didn't want you to hire me?"

"Paul's girlfriend, Lisa. She thinks it was you still. That's what she keeps telling everyone. She won't listen to me."

"Thanks for the vote of confidence."

"So how do I find out if it was really them?"

"The cops find out if it was really them. Whoever 'them' is."

"Cops suck, man."

"For the most part I agree. But it is their job to find and arrest murderers."

"No, that's not fucking good enough, man. Some fucking cop told Lisa there wasn't much to go on; that they think it may be a random mugging. So I don't have that much confidence in the cops. And this is not fair. There's got to be some--"

"Nothing's fair, kid. The world's rigged. If Jensen was a friend, he wouldn't want you to go on some half-assed vendetta."

"He's got a year old baby at home and Lisa. It isn't nothing that he's gone. Someone murdered him for a reason. I want to know who and why. And you can help me."

"No, I can't. Even if I tried, I wouldn't. You're better off--"

"Man, please--"

"I... I don't even know your name."

"I'm Ron."

I wasn't feeling particularly sympathetic to Ron's cause. But I was exhausted with batting him down, and I didn't have the energy to keep dumping on someone so miserable.

"I'll go with you to Benny's. Just to talk. I'll try to get him to slip or incriminate himself or whatever. Maybe that brings you some peace. But that's all I'm willing to do. Just--"

"Awesome. Yeah, that's great. Are we going now?"

"Sure. Do you like the subway, Ron?"

We took a cab to Chena Pan. Ron paid. The kid and I walked in. There were almost no patrons. Benny sat at a back table with the two thugs he brought to my dinner. Wedged in between the degenerates were two girls far too young to be in the company of such undistinguished gentlemen.

"Detective Graves, smart move, man. It's good you came."

"I'm still quit, Benjamin."

"Fine, but where is the girl?"

"My friend and I have some questions."

"Graves, you're working for me, you're not working for me, you're here, you're there... Stop playing fucking games and tell me what I want to know."

"We've been through this. I can't find her. Now, why don't you tell me why you were fucking with Paul Jensen?"

"I don't know any Paul Jensen."

The kid was anxious and unwisely spoke out of turn.

"Yes, you do."

"I don't know Paul Jensen. And I don't know you."

"You didn't know him, but you were willing to kill him."

"Ha-ha. Please get the fuck out of here. Graves, you and this kid going to try and pin a murder wrap on me. You're hanging around with too many fucking junkies, man."

Ron spat out a "Fuck you."

Benny didn't take it well.

"Fuck me? Fuck me? Hey, fuck you. Fuck you. You and your whole fucking crew of rich spoiled, thumb sucking fucks. Where the fuck would you be without us? Scoring dimes on corners and scared shitless. And look how you repay us. You want to know about Paul Jensen? Paul Jensen was a dumb fuck that got exactly what he deserved. Just like you will and Heather will and Sam will and--"

"You did kill him, you piece of shit."

"Get the fuck out of my restaurant, you fucking yuppie."

At this point everyone one of the lackeys at Benny's table was screaming at Ron. I kept him a safe distance away. Benny's parents were also screaming in Chinese. The few patrons of the restaurant were making for the exit. I was anxious to follow.

I grabbed Ron's shirt and shoved him towards the door.

"Wait outside."

Ron straightened his shirt and marched outside. Through the windows, I could see him resting up against the fire hydrant.

"I can't believe you brought--"

"Shut the fuck up, Benny. You are so dumb. That kid has some stories. Stories he's probably going to start telling the police."

"He doesn't know shit."

"You better hope so. Goodbye, Benny."

"Wait… He wants to talk to you. Face to face."

"He?"

"You know."

"Well the Prince of Punks can--"

"You really have no fucking idea what all this is all about. Rolando wants to talk with you. He'll pay out if--"

"Thanks for the offer but--"

"Here. This is like three or four grand. You wait here. Rolando will be come by and you can talk here. You just got to listen. Take the money. You ain't never going to make four grand quicker."

"He's here in fifteen minutes or I am not."

"I feel you."

"Feel your way to a phone. I'm going to go talk to the kid."

Benny motioned to one of his disciples for a cell phone. I walked outside to talk with the kid. He was pacing, finishing a cigarette.

"Did he tell you anything else?"

"Kid, you got as good a confession out of him as I can possibly imagine anyone on earth getting out of him."

"Yeah but why? Paul didn't rob them."

"Ron--"

"Paulie just introduced them to Heather. That's it."

"Ron, it's a murder, not rocket science. It's not hard to figure out. It's simple and awful. Benny killed or had Paulie killed because it was beneficial."

"How was it beneficial?"

"Hey, you can kill yourself trying to understand every facet of the circle of life or you can accept it. Your friend is dead. That guy is probably behind it. One way or another. And if you don't want to end up like Paul, then you need to go home and tuck away all that shit you got stewing. Those feelings will turn you into a young corpse."

"Fine. Fine. Fine. What are you going to do?"

"I'm going to stick around here for a bit and talk with

Benny's boss."

"Fuck that. If Rolando's coming here, man, I want to talk to him too."

"I mean, Ron, shut up. This is nearly unmanageable for me. And I've been involved in this same kind of game with these same morons before. It's not a fun sandbox to play in."

"Okay. Okay. But I can't do nothing. I can't go home."

"Fine. Go back to my office. I'll be back in a bit. We'll go to the cops together. We'll get 'em squared away. Then, they'll take it from there. Okay?"

He nodded. I patted him on the shoulder and said, "Good. Finish your cigarette and go."

Ron trudged off. He was oblivious to the gaming. He was out for justice. And there's no place for that in criminal worlds. Inside Chena Pan, Benny and his boys were standing at attention.

"We'll take you to see Rolando."

"We can meet here."

Benny's lackeys' hands emerged from their pockets. Each had a gangster roll. Each handed it to Benny. Benny clasped all three rolls together in one hand. He closed one eye and peered at the girth of all the cash.

"That's seven grand easy. No strings. You just got to get in the car and go for a five-minute ride. Rolando can't meet us here."

"Either you're a terrible fucking businessman, stupid enough to think that seven grand will entice me to a one-way ticket down the east river or--"

"He wants see you. That's it. I swear."

"Maybe. You got a car."

"It's parked right out front."

"You packing?"

"Never."

"Lift up your shirt and twirl for me."

Benny lifted up his shirt and spun around. The he lifted up each pant leg. He didn't appear to be armed.

"Satisfied, Detective?"

"No. You drive. All the girlfriends stay here."

One of the guys tossed Benny the keys to the car. Benny marched past me. The car was a big Lincoln Navigator; waxed to a mirror shine. Benny entered quickly. I hesitated, mumbling something along the lines of 'Fuck. I wish I had a gun.'

I got in the passenger seat and immediately pulled out my cell phone. I was casually looking around the car, searching the glove box and whatnot when Renee picked up her cell phone.

"Hey. I'm on my way back."

"I'm in a car right now with our friend Benny C."

"Why?"

"Money mostly. We're in a black Lincoln Navigator with plates CGH – 129 and we're headed to meet up with our friend Rolando Pequeno. I just wanted to let you know, in case I end up missing or anything. You should tell the cops I went to meet Rolando at…"

Benny slammed the glove compartment shut. I was looking through it. He snarled out, "Building on the corner of 112th and 3rd "

I echoed the information into the phone. Renee was apprehensive.

"Graves, I don't like the sound of this. Should I call Pierce?"

"No. It's just a friendly chat, but feel free to send an army after me if I don't return this afternoon."

"Be smart."

CHAPTER TWELVE

It was a short ride to his run down building on the corner of York. We took a suspiciously creaky elevator to the fourth floor. The windows were covered in newspaper. Light jabbed through rips in the paper. I could see three people with Rolando in the glass-encased office at the end of the floor. Another three guys played video games on couches outside the office. They were unfazed by my presence. Their soccer video game took precedence.

Benny opened the door to Rolando's makeshift office. There were wires streaming across the cement floor and one Persian rug in the middle of the room. He had an antique desk adorned with a small lamp, a few cell phones and a computer. Two of his men were trying to fix a florescent ceiling light on one side of the room. The ladder was shaking underneath them. Rolando was rattling off orders and bitching when I stepped in.

"Changing light bulbs may be asking too much."

Rolando was going for a mature power broker look, but it was a tough sell. He looked uneasy behind a desk, and he didn't have the right shoes for the role. He was flustered the second I stepped into the room.

"You two get fucking down. You can fix it later."

"Rolando Pequeno. P-E-Q-U-E-N-O. Prince of Punks finally made it."

"It's pronounced Pequeno, but why don't you call me Rolando instead and I'll call you Graves instead of bitch."

"Okay. You'll have to forgive me, godfather."

"Benny paid you to find Heather Lawson."

"No, he paid a retainer. So I looked for Heather Lawson. But I did not find Heather Lawson. So I quit to save you guys some money. Put it towards the next g-pack or some office furniture."

"That's not going to work for me."

"I don't care."

One of Rolando's many problems was that he got emotional. He would get worked-up and huff and puff and try to blow your house down. He liked to cry and whine, especially to his mother and uncle. Rolando's mother was a gentle woman, though her brother was not. And Rolando's father was never mistaken for a gentle man. He was Brazilian. He came to the states to get away from someone or something. He was high-class muscle in Summers' crew before knocking up Summers' sister. Then when Rolando was young, his father got hit with a seven-year stretch. He never made it out of prison. I'm sure his demise was for the better, in respect to society at large, but Rolando took it hard. His uncle certainly didn't soften the blow. So Rolando had some baggage and was quick to get emotional. Usually, he didn't get the kind of emotional that lead to smart-ass private detectives dying. At least that's what I was thinking.

"Fuck you, Graves. You can't quit."

"I can and I did."

"What I mean is you're not quit."

"I don't give a shit what you mean, Rolando."

"Name a price."

"You aren't rich enough."

"Cut the fucking shit, motherfucker. You're a dealer. Always have been. What the fuck do you want?"

"Do me and the world a favor and crawl back to--"

"I'll give you thirty grand to deliver her to me today."

"If this is why you wanted to see, you wasted a lot of your boys' money."

I cracked my neck and got up to leave.

"I didn't say you could fucking leave."

"I didn't fucking ask."

Two guys stood in front of the door. I wasn't going to move them.

"What's the matter Graves? You don't like bribes now that you ain't a cop. That's fucking backwards. As a civilian motherfucker, you should be more game for this shit. So I'm thinking--"

"Don't think. It ain't your strong suit. And besides, you can't start now. You've got a rep to uphold."

"I'm thinking that you may need to call Heather for me. Right now."

"Rolando, I'm not helping you. I'm leaving. People know I'm here."

I looked over as Benny nodded to Rolando in agreement with my statement. Then I continued on berating Rolando.

"And I'm confident you're just going to watch me leave, because you wouldn't want cops coming by and checking on you... here with all these 'known' criminals. That would just fuck up your whole day; you getting remanded back into custody on such a nice summer day. It'd be a damn shame. ...And while I'm on the subject, how did you manage to get out so early? You sliced off a lot of years."

"Good lawyer. Good behavior."

"More like a good rolling story to a good Federal agent."

"I never roll."

I turned to the two guys blocking the door. I put my hand on one of the guy's shoulder. They slowly parted. Rolando followed me out of the office, saying, "You should know that I ain't letting you or Heather make me look like some punk ass bitch."

" 'Course not. We wouldn't want to take your job away from you."

"I will collect heads if I have to."

I exited with his threats still lofting around behind me like bad gas and headed south. I called the office to relieve Renee's anxiety. Hal picked up.

"Uh. Graves Investigations"

"You have a sensual telephone voice."

"Hey ass hole, you do have clients, you know? You should've seen how fucking nutty this last bone head was."

"You can handle the next appointment by yourself can't you?"

"Yeah. Where do you keep the standard contracts?"

"You have to print them out from the computer."

"Oh fuck."

"Just wait for Renee. She should be back any second."

"Okay. Where are you going?"

"I've got to settle up with my bookie and I thought I might grab a real nice lunch while I'm at it."

"That's nice. I'll see ya when you decide to start working for a living again."

I made it to Sal's spot quick. His office, if you could call it that, was above a shitty bar on the lower east side. It smelled like dead fish all the fucking time. But he got some pretty high rollers up stairs from time to time. He moved his place around a lot but I had still lost many a penny to that man and in that room. Sharpe was inhaling a nuclear sized submarine sandwich when I walked in.

"Jesus, Sharpe. At least make an effort to make it past forty."

He flicked me off and continued eating. There was a craps game going on. Sal was playing in it. He had just rolled a bust. He had gray hair, a large potbelly and suspenders. He was sweating. He rolled down his sleeves, picked up a few dollars and threw them back in his pockets.

"Ya know, I've been fucking waiting on you. You finally settling up?"

"Yeah. So aren't you happy to see me?"

"Ecstatic. You do have the money on you, I hope. The Orioles lost too you know."

"Oh. At least they're doing what they're good at."

I pulled out my gangster's roll. I broke off seventeen hundred and handed it over. Sal started to get real excited.

"Business is good, I take it. What's your secret?"

"Being the only guy in the room with a middle school education. "

"I'll have to remember that. Stick around. The game is rolling real nice. You might pick up a few more dollars."

"You must take me for a real sucker, Sally boy."

"Who me?"

"Yeah, you."

"Nooooo. You're my idol. I just want to see you roll a couple. You've gone on some rolls before."

"Not today"

"Come now."

"It's rolling nice?"

"Oh yeah!"

"Well, I can't take your word for it. I should find out for myself."

I took off my coat and rolled three winners in a row. I came in with sixty three hundred in cash. I paid out seventeen. Then I put some money on sevens. I made a few good rolls. Then I put my money on a hard eight. And I walked out with about ten grand. I nearly doubled my money in less then twenty minutes. Things were really looking up there for a moment.

I grabbed a bite to eat at a deli and took a cab to the office. The taxi driver didn't pull up quite far enough.

"The cops have got the street blocked off. This is as close as I can get ya."

"What?"

"Look they got it all blocked off. $14.15."

I got out a hundred without taking my eyes off the blockade. I mumbled, "Keep it" and jumped out.

It was the only time in my life I left a 600% tip, but I was preoccupied. The entire block in front of my building was barricaded off. It was no accident. Somebody had done something on purpose. And I had the feeling the something had be done to my office or the people in my office. I approached the barricade. My pace quickened. There were two ambulances, a fire truck and over a half dozen patrol cars. Lights were flashing everywhere. I spotted a uniform directing bystanders.

"Hey! Hey! Where's the lead detective?"

"Sir stand back, move away--"

"That's my office over there. Graves Investigations, second floor. I'm Graves."

"That's your office?"

"Yeah"

"Let me get Hope of over here for you. Sgt. Simmons, I've got a Mr. Graves over here. He says this is his office over here. You want to tell Detective Hope?"

"What happened?"

"Hold on."

"The lead detective will be over to talk--"

Taking in the sites: the shaking heads, the bustling, the coffees being passed around, the crowd control and all the tape; I knew there were bodies. I had this picture in my mind. I saw my office door still open, blood spatters against over the walls, and her corpse. I saw her clothes saturated in blood, clinging to her skin. I saw her face expressionless. I saw her hands dangling at her sides. It all came to me at once. I felt it all run up and down my spine a million times. I couldn't will myself to breathe.

When I started to talk again, it didn't feel like a conversation. I didn't feel like anyone was around.

"How many bodies?"

"Sir, I don't--"

"I used to be on the job. C'mon."

"It's a triple."

"Did they pull 'em out yet?"

"No. No one knows what happened. If you just hold on--"

"Move out of my way."

Hope appeared out of the abyss of lights, marching hastily.

"Graves, tell me you know what the fuck happened here--Let him fucking through."

"He said it's a triple."

"Yeah. It's not pretty."

I said, "Renee" to myself, still not able to fully grasp that I was in a conversation. Hope burst my bubble, aggressively jumping back into the questioning.

"What? Who's Renee?"

"The woman."

"What woman?"

"What woman? My secretary. The woman laying--"

"You have a female secretary?"

"What kind of fucking question is that? Who the fuck do you think is--"

"I got three male DOAs. And as for your secretary, that's a new mystery for me."

My lungs started to work again. In the midst of total chaos and dread, I have to admit the sudden realization that she wasn't one of those bodies was probably the greatest I've ever had. It pains me to admit that was my reaction to three senseless murders, but I've never known a better relief.

"You checked the whole building?"

"Yeah. We cleared it. Two were in your office. One was waiting on the couch. Where the fuck were you?"

"I--uh ...Ha-Ha. I had lunch. Where could she be?"

"Who? I don't know. Where? You got a receipt?"

"A receipt?"

"To show me where and when you had fucking lunch?"

"Uh…No. Who are the D.O.A.'s?"

"Stein's getting the IDs now. That's four bodies now."

"Shit. Hal, that fucking kid…damn it. I should've fucking known--"

"Hal who? What kid?"

"Hal Dyson. He used to be on the job. He was helping me with some cases."

"Not anymore. Who's the kid?"

"The kid, I just met. His name is Ron. I just met him."

"Last name?"

"I…I honestly don't know."

"This is not looking good, Graves."

"Where could she be? If he took her--I fucking can't believe that twofaced, Brazilian, cock-sucking maggot."

"Slow up. Who are you talking about? I don't know who you're talking about."

"What the fuck does it matter to you?"

"Graves, I am not fucking around. This is a triple homicide. You will tell me everything you know. I decide if it's pertinent."

"Rolando Pequeno. P-e-q-u-e-n-o. Got released from Otisville recently. I helped send him away around 2000 and he was looking at 10 years no matter what. But he's out. Fuck. Where is Renee?"

"Give me a description of this girl."

"Brunette, five foot eight. She was wearing blue coat--"

"Oh. Uniforms on the other side of the block have a girl in the back of one of the squad cars. We can't get a coherent sentence out of her. I thought she--"

I checked two squad cars before finding her. Renee was shaking. She wasn't crying, but obviously had been. Her legs were dangling out of the back of a squad car. She was intently staring at the face of our building.

"Renee…Renee"

"You fucking ass hole. What the fuck--"

I pulled her up and out of the backseat. Her head was on my chest as she muttered, "What the fuck did you do? ...What the fuck did you do?"

"... Nothing"

Stein and Hope broke up our moment. Stein began reciting the information from his notepad.

"The D.O.A.s are Hal Dyson, retired sergeant, Ronald Bass, a 24 year from the west side and a Jonathan Gonetti, from Riverside? Ring any bells?"

"Gonetti made an appointment for 3 o'clock. Hal was going to handle it. Bass was a friend of Paul Jensen."

A patrolman yelled that CSU was almost finished. Stein who had been trying to read me, broke off to talk to an officer in a CSU jacket.

"You two are going to have to come down to the house."

"Yeah..."

The coroners van pulled up. Another van pulled in right behind it. Three sets of men went up carrying three stretchers with black padding. I figured the stretchers wouldn't be so easy to carry down.

I didn't stay to see them come back down. I slid into the back of a patrol car. Renee did the same. Her crutches sat in the middle. We went down to the station.

Renee sat in a chair outside one of the interview rooms while I sat inside the room. Hope bent down and gave her a glass of water. He knew to handle her differently than he did me. He said, "Detective Stein is going to be back in a few minutes to get your statement."

She nodded, still struggling to digest whatever she had taken in.

The interview room wasn't much different than it had been ten years before when I had last entered it. There was staleness about it. I sat down still able to see Renee, wide eyed and scared in her chair, her crutches on the ground next to her. Hope slammed the door shut.

"Who goes into a homicidal rage at three in the

afternoon in midtown?"

"I'll tell ya when I know myself."

"The canvases better come up real helpful and you better too. This is not going to be quick and painless."

I cracked my neck, knowing full well Hope wasn't lying.

Hours later I exited the room to find Renee in the same spot. A coffee was in her hand but it didn't look as if he she'd taken a sip.

"Let's go."

"They're letting you go?"

"I didn't do anything, Renee. We can go."

"Was it that guy Benny?"

"I don't know. I don't think so. But I don't know. They'll find out."

"They'll find out? What about you? …Don't you care?"

"About what?"

"About what? How about the three men that just got murdered in cold blood? Jesus, Graves, don't you have a soul."

"Calm down."

"Why? You're calm enough for the both of us."

"Fine. Yell all you want. I don't give a shit. But there's nothing for me to do aside from get you out of here."

"How can you be so cold?"

"Because it keeps me warm at night"

"You have a very fucked up perspective on the value of human life."

"Okay. Let's go."

"No. I'm not going--"

"You either come with me or you go into protective custody with them."

"Where are you going to go?"

"Staten Island."

Renee reluctantly moved towards the cab. She was half using her crutches for about two steps. Then she threw them ten feet down the sidewalk. I left them there and followed her into the cab. Pierce picked us up from the ferry and brought us back to his house.

Once inside, Renee whisked past us. Margie beckoned for her. I looked at Pierce blankly. There was a tacit understanding that the shitty-ness of the situation made for little conversation. I shut the door behind myself.

"You two can stay for however long you need to."

"It won't be that long."

"What makes you say that?"

"Well, he fucked up. Four homicides. All around Midtown. He's royally fucked now."

"Rolando is out of his--"

"Ha-ha. Rolando."

"What?"

"He's not that indiscriminate even when he's emotional. Not even the wannabe gangsters that Rolando employs have the balls to walk into midtown in broad daylight and pop off 15 rounds."

"The perp was probably looking for you."

"Yeah, Hope said he hit this kid, Ron first. He took two in the chest, two in the leg. He was sitting in the couch near Renee's desk. I figure once this guy hit Ron, he didn't hesitate to walk in and hit the others... even when the fuck opened the door and found poor fucking Hal and some mope with a two timing wife."

"This is bad, Graves."

"Fuck it. Everybody's looking at me like I'm wearing a big 'guilty motherfucker' sign. I'm sorry it happened, but I ain't apologizing and I ain't guilty. I didn't pull any triggers. I want these fuckers just as bad as anyone else."

"Graves, let me save you some thinking. Because I know you're going to start thinking about this far more than you should. You aren't a hero. And you aren't nearly as smart as you think you are. I love you, brother, but you're ordinary. You aren't superman. You're going to die, but the luxury afforded to you presently, is that you get to choose when and where. You loose that luxury if you go out and try to play hero. You aren't built for it. Hey, look at me... and listen to me. There isn't any day to save. Sit down and have some dinner with Renee. Lay low. Weather the storm."

"I don't want to eat Margie's food, Pierce."

"Of course you don't, but we're suffering together tonight. Smells great, babe."

I laughed at Pierce. He slapped me on the back a few times. He was good at shaking off the atrocities of the world. I was usually better; something gained from murder scenes being former daily customs. Margie was burning something and two daughters were watching TV. Pierce hovered behind Margie and rested his head on her shoulder

"Sweetheart, here let me help you with the salad."

"Ha-ha. Get off of me, you ape. You smell like criminals. Go sit over there. See Renee, at least Graves doesn't get handsy."

Renee looked at me with a blank expression.

"No, he doesn't", Renee said, frankly.

Margie and Pierce persisted with their aged puppy love act much to my chagrin. Renee and I sat a seat apart at dinner. We didn't speak much. I recounted the story of the day to Margie and Pierce fully. I didn't embellish much or decorate the story with small details and personal opinions. I spit it out, boring and tragic. It was a bad story. It was cold. I thought by sparing Renee the details that I was somehow saving her a certain amount of anguish. In actuality, I was inflicting more as I did things like describe Ron to Margie. Renee wasn't as distraught over the senseless killings as she was of my reactions and feelings about the senseless killings. She cared about me more than the guys who died. Renee had thought I was dead when she saw the lights and the cars at the office. I couldn't fully appreciate what that was like for her. I was so happy to find her alive that I forgot everything else. She had a better memory.

I excused myself as Renee, Margie and Pierce polished off the second bottle of wine. I made a quick phone call. I returned to Renee clearing dishes.

"Who'd you call?"

"No one"

She shook her head in disapproval. She threw the dishes into the sink and turned on the water.

The guest room was a nasty, poorly furnished basement with an old pull out couch. Pierce brought some blankets and pillows down.

"The pullout is terrible for your back, but it's—well--."

Renee was attempting to act gracious, thanking Pierce and taking the pillows and blankets from him.

"Thanks, pal."

"Okay. Goodnight, then."

The door to the upstairs shut. I helped Renee pull the cushions off the sofa and make the bed.

"You okay?"

She didn't respond. I tried to evoke a response a few times. They were fruitless endeavors. The bed was made when she finally spoke.

"I think I'm going to take a blanket and sleep on the couch upstairs."

"Hey…Hold on."

"Don't touch me."

"Fine. Look, I'm not staying."

"What?"

"I'm leaving."

"To go where?"

"I have to straighten some things out."

"What? What are you talking about? You said…"

Renee put her arms up to keep me at arms length. She turned her head too, as I had reached in to kiss her. She continually tried to push me away. I roughly brought her in close and kissed her on the cheek. Her arms were squeezed in between our bodies. Her anger didn't dissipate with a kiss.

"Get away from me."

"Whatever you say. Here. Hold on to this for me."

I broke out my wad. I had to forcefully put it into her hands.

"Take it."

"No. Wait. Wait. Graves, you can't go."

I was turning the knob on the backdoor when I stopped for a moment. I turned my head over my shoulder to say,

"Don't go anywhere. It's not an order or a command. It's a plea. Please don't go anywhere."

"Where—Wait. Where are you going, Graves?"

The door clattered behind me, stifling her last words.

CHAPTER THIRTEEN

The taxi driver was waiting on the other side of the street with his lights off per my request.

"Thanks for waiting. Manhattan, Charles Street"

I couldn't remember the exact address. I thought it was 37 or 73. I had the cabby drop me off on the corner of Bleecker and Charles and started hunting. I went up the odd side of the block looking at the registers on the buttons. The third townhouse I checked was 67. S. Carlson lived on the third floor. I started ringing her bell. No one answered. I buzzed 1A incessantly. The door to the first floor apartment opened. A young black woman in a bathrobe looked out. I held my card against the glass for her to see.

"What's this about?"

"I apologize. I had an appointment with someone who lives in this building. Sam Carlson."

"Ah... Do you know what time it is?"

"Yeah. 12:25. I'm a private investigator. Any idea--"

"3b. The girls' apartment with the music and the smoke?"

"Probably"

"Yeah, I don't know them. Goodnight."

"Anything could be helpful?"

"I don't know her. Please leave the building."

"Okay. Yeah. Wait, what? Her?"

"Sam Carlson?"

"Yeah. Sam Carlson."

"Sam Carlson, blonde, female, this tall. Her."

"Fuck. Yeah. That would make sense. Samantha Carlson"

"You're a detective?"

"Not a very good one, evidently"

"Yeah, well she lives in 3b with another girl."

"A blonde, this high, looks kind of strung out?"

"Yeah, I guess and the little boy. I've got to get back to bed."

"Yeah. Thanks. I'm just going to go knock on her door. Wait! Little boy?"

"Go and knock if you want. Don't rob anybody. I can pick you out of a lineup if I have to."

The door for 3b was on my left. The smell was creeping down the stairway. On closer inspection it looked like a crowbar and a shoulder had been taken to the door recently. It wouldn't shut properly. I pushed it open. I didn't hear anything at first. The rooms were dark. No lights were on. I cracked my neck.

I knew not to follow that smell. I knew to turn around and run. Before I could, the door slammed into me and I spun around to stare down the barrel of hand cannon.

"Don't say a fucking word, bitch."

I complied and I moved around to the middle of the room as another hood leapt out from the bedroom.

"Who the fuck are you?"

"A friend of Sam's. We had a date. She stood me up. It's not a big deal. I'll just leave."

The hand cannon wielder cut me off before I could move back out the door.

"Motherfucker, don't move. Where do I know you from?"

"I'm an actor. I'm on TV all the time. Every sitcom, every CSI, you name it I've been on it. I'm real recognizable."

"No. No. Ruiz where do I know this guy from?"

The guy from the bedroom came around to look me in the face. He struggled to place my face. I didn't have the same problem. I recognized them right away. The hand cannon operator had been outside the restaurant when Benny interrupted my date. The other guy had been playing the video game at Rolando's building.

"I don't know, man. Let's go. 5-0 could show up. I don't want to be in this fucking place, man. Not with the fucking body in there. It stinks."

The lanky lackey left a trail of bloody boot prints across the room.

"Nah, man. I know this fucking guy."

"Let's go."

I interjected.

"It smells like we should all leave."

"Nobody's talking to you, holmes."

"Okay. Okay. I don't want to get caught here either. Why don't we all just go our separate--"

"I remember. You're that old cop. He was the one that pissed off Ro this morning."

"Nah, man. He ain't a cop. He got tossed for being dirty or something. He does like cop work for regular people."

"Processor server"

I butted in as the stupidity of the two men became too much to handle and it was obvious even with their severely limited intelligence they knew who I was.

"I'm a fucking private detective. Good God."

The hand cannon encroached. The lanky idiot was nervous and it showed.

"C'mon we got to get the fuck out of here. Forget about this fool."

"Nah. Rolando's pissed now man. The cops are

looking for him everywhere and shit. Nah, this guy is coming with us."

"Fine, man. But let's fucking go."

I couldn't resist the urge to fuck with the idiots.

"Yeah. Let's boogey."

"You a comedian?"

"Not a professional like you"

The gun hand ushered me through the door. The other idiot hurried down the three flights of stairs and rocketed out the door. He looked both ways down the street. He was in the car before we were out the door.

"I've got ten grand in cash in Staten Island. All yours--"

"We ain't dirty like you. We got some honor."

"Oh, I'm glad you got that."

"Get in the mother fucking car."

I got in the back of the car.

Rolando was frazzled when we arrived.

"I got cops crawling all over every fucking place I go. My house, my building, my girl's place. What the fuck did you do to me, Graves?"

"Me? You brought this shit on yourself."

"SHUT THE FUCK UP! And give me a straight answer."

"You had three people killed this afternoon."

"The fuck I did. You can't tie me to shit. You've got them out to get me, motherfucker. They'll violate my ass right back to O-ville."

"One can only hope"

"Who was the dead girl in Carlson's apartment?"

"How should I fucking know?"

"Carlson?"

"No fucking idea."

"They say the girls face was bashed in. Wasn't fucking me. I've had people hanging outside that apartment for a week waiting for Carlson. I told them to bust in the door tonight and they find one long dead bitch. So I'm asking you for the last time. Where is Heather Lawson, Graves? Because if that bitch doesn't appear, you're ass is fucking found dead and puffy in the river next month. So tell me."

"Yeah, well, even though I would so enjoy a good swim, I've been telling you for fucking days that I don't know where she is. But I will tell you this for certain: This is going to end bad and bloody unless you give it up now. Start running. Forget the drugs, the money, the girl, whatever you have to... and run like hell."

Rolando started to giggle like a madman on the verge of a spectacular breakdown. I laughed at him until he took a gun out and cocked it back.

"Put that away. You're only going to scare yourself."

"You don't know what you're doing. You think you're smarter than me... You think you're better than me. You're not. You're shit. And I ain't. I'm going to get mine."

"Rolando--"

A phone rang loudly. It wasn't a dire situation yet and I could've gotten a stay of execution various ways, but the phone call was welcomed. The lanky lackey picked up the phone.

"Ro, it's Benny."

Rolando grabbed the phone. He passed off the gun, devoting his full attention to the telephone. I cracked my neck and took a full breath.

"Yo... Good. ...NO. You wait right there. I'm coming there now. Yeah, you wait."

He came back over to me.

"Guess you didn't look in the right places."

I was escorted inside a new vehicle. This time it was a perfectly waxed SUV. It was probably two am when we pulled up next to Benny's very similar transport. Rolando exited before we reached a full stop.

"Make sure he doesn't go anywhere."

I couldn't make out anyone in the other car or anything going on in the other car. After forty-five seconds Rolando exited the other car on one side and Benny exited on the other side. Rolando was furious, ranting in Portuguese. It put a smile on my face.

Rolando was directing Benny to do something with a flurry of hand motions and finger pointing. He slammed the door as he got back in the car.

"Was she hiding under the bed or in the--"

"Graves, not another fucking word or I will snap. I will snap and I will fucking kill you. I will."

I shut up, and continued to smile. Watching him in so much agony was nearly as pleasing as inflicting it myself.

"I want all your files on the Lawson's."

"Files? I don't keep files on these people. Give it up. Let me go home. Whoever you have in that car can definitely be more helpful than I can."

"Take you home. That's a good idea."

"...I'll get out here. Save you the trip."

"Nah. We want to see your place. Check out the furniture. So what's the address?"

"If you think I'm telling you that, you're certifiably retarded."

It was three am when I opened the door to my apartment. I ushered them all into my living room. Most of them had pistols in the back of their pants. The pistols were more noticeable as I deemed Rolando's desperation and anger to be genuine and mounting. He was far past his usual emotional self, teetering on treacherous.

"I'd rather you not touch anything... you know, health precautions."

A creek sounded down the hallway towards the bedroom. Three pulled guns. I wanted it to be a clamoring pipe. But I knew I wasn't that lucky and I figured it was her.

"Bringing your work home with you?"

"...Shit."

The punks were perplexed. One pointed out, "That's

not Lawson."

I shook my head, winced and rubbed my palms against my eyes. I cracked my neck.

"Nope. Welcome home, babe."

Rolando's grin spanned from one ear to the other.

"Mrs. Graves…"

The thugs spread out over the apartment. They wondered around aimlessly. Mary and I were sitting on the couch with the hand cannon-wielding moron across from us.

Rolando was holding one of my half empty bottles of whiskey.

"Make yourself one for the road."

"But I like it here. These chairs and shit. It's nice. Real nice."

"Leave us alone and go bother Heather."

"You best believe I'm going to track her down and do just that, but I got this like overwhelming feeling you know more than you're telling me… and now your wife is here and I'm thinking you're going to be more cooperative."

"Anybody can disappear, Rolando. It can be done. It's very easy with 450 grand too."

"It's not about the 450."

"Than what the fuck does-- Fuck it. I don't want to know."

"You don't want to know?"

"No, like I have been trying to tell you. This does not concern me."

"Sure does, because you know things… like about the 450. Things you ain't telling me."

"I know she ripped you off. I know she's looking for Michael Lawson. I know her father wont have anything to do with her. And I know you or your uncle is pissed enough to kill over this."

"Let's hope it don't go that far."

His grin stretched from ear to ear.

"Peoples just don't like you, Graves. I get that now. You ain't that cool. At least not as cool as you think you is."

He pushed his gun up to my face. I slapped it away.

"You think I won't pull the trigger!"

"I think you won't pull the trigger."

"See lady, your husband doesn't show me due respect. He might not be smart enough to want to live but maybe you are. So I suggest you get him to shut the fuck up and start showing me some respect."

Mary processed Rolando's advice. "You want him to shut up or keep talking, respectfully?"

Mary had inadvertently pissed Rolando off even more. My grin stretched from ear to ear. He was such a pathetic little creature. I couldn't bear to keep my mouth shut.

"You're such a little bitch. You know that?"

He pivoted around and pistol-whipped me. I went out like a light. The doctor told me later if that blow had been just a few centimeters to the left or if Rolando had been a little stronger, there would've been no tomorrow.

I came to with dried blood down the left side of my face. My feet, hands and torso had been duct taped in an especially disorganized manner. It looked like they had attempted to mummify me with tape. I moaned for a minute or two before fully coming around.

"I see your head moving, Rupert. I know you can hear me now. Wake up!"

"Jesus, I feel like a fucking mummy. Did they leave?"

"No. They brought some more company for us too."

Heather was bound with tape over her mouth. She was taped to the stool next to the kitchen counter.

"Heather, nice of you to finally join us."

She gave me a hostile glare. Mary started in on me again, saying, "Is your head still bleeding?"

"I don't know. I can't really feel much right now."

"Does it feel like it's still bleeding?"

"What did I just say? Why are you here?"

"I see. I wasn't aware I was so unwelcome. And I didn't exactly expect you to be immersed in some kind of hostage crisis at our apartment."

"Crisis? This is a small misunderstanding, but I am hoping they shoot me soon."

"This is not a funny situation, Rupert"

"No shit, Mary."

"As we are being held hostage by five deranged drug dealers, I don't find this to be any kind of a laughing matter. In fact, the gravity of the situation may lend itself to you taking this fucking seriously."

"No, my head hurts. I refuse to use it."

Mary was furiously trying either to free herself or to hit me. I can't be sure which she wanted to do more. I took a few long deep breaths. There was an empty glass atop some papers on the coffee table. I used my heel to tip the table. The glass wobbled, stubbornly. But after a second, it tumbled to the ground. I shimmied around until I could reach the glass with my feet. I rolled it closer to me, and stabilized it.

"Who are these guys? What are they doing here? ...What are you doing?"

I stomped down on it. The cup didn't break into many pieces, but a long vertical piece cracked off, leaving a jagged edge. I started jostling around until the tape around my ankle began to tear. When I finished with the tape around my feet, I put the glass between my feet.

"Rupert, you're going to shut up now? You are such a child. You have absolutely no consideration for others. You are completely ignorant to the fact that your actions, your attitude and your words affect--"

I had gotten through enough of the tape to free my hands. I proceeded to un-mummify myself and ask Mary, "Would you like me to un-tape you?"

"Please."

I cut the tape off Mary and then took the tape off Heather's mouth.

"He is going to do something even stupider if you don't give him everything he wants."

"I don't have the money."

"What about--"

There was a rustling and voices near the door. I grabbed a knife from the kitchen counter. I cut the rest of the tape off Heather.

"Fire escape"

The girls quietly filed over to the window next to the fire escape. Mary had the window open. Heather exited first, trying to make as little noise as possible. Mary was out on the fire escape whispering, "Rupert. Rupert, what are you doing?"

"My dad's gun in the bedroom. Go ahead"

"No"

"Just go."

I took a step away from the window when I heard the door crack open. I immediately jumped through the window and followed Mary down the stairs. I fell and made a racket tumbling down. By the time I was at the ladder I could see Benny exiting the window and heading down after us.

"GRAVES! GRAVES!"

I got my cell phone out before I hit the ground with 911 dialed. We were in the alley next to my apartment and running towards the street when they picked up.

"911 Emergency services."

"A cop's been shot on the corner of--Trace the call--"

The man with the hand cannon came around the corner with his gun to Heather's head, and said, "Drop the fucking phone."

I abided.

"That was fucking stupid, Graves."

Rolando came out of my building. Flustered and anxious, he was losing it with every passing second.

"Not here. Get them the fuck inside."

"Rolando… Benny, c'mon. Let's bargain."

Rolando, the hand cannon man and one other punk all had guns drawn. We moved as a large pack into the lobby. I was struck by the sudden impression that I blew by our last exit.

I tried to reason with them, stating, "This is... unmanageable" as we moved inside. Rolando stopped the pack. Violently, he slapped Heather across the face. Her face was already a bit beaten up and that slap left another large red mark across her face.

"You fucked it all up."

As Rolando uttered the last syllable, there was a barrage of whooshes from the doorway. Before I could turn my head to identify the sound's origin, bodies hit the ground.

I pulled Mary in. We huddled against the wall. I saw the hand cannon wielder take a bullet to the throat and collapse. Heather was on the other side of the hall with her hands over her head. Bits of Rolando's head were over the wall above her. His bloody face laid on the floor, facing Mary and me. The hand cannon wielder ended up face down; so did the others. And for a moment, I heard nothing.

Then something squeaked down the hall. Benny pulled himself towards the stairs, only able to use one arm. The trail of blood behind him grew wider and deeper with every inch of his crawl.

The shooter passed right by us. I saw his shoes first, then his pressed, black pants. I didn't want to see anymore. He dropped the clip out of his pistol. It clanked on the tile. I shuttered at the crash, looking up to see a ski mask and flat, green eyes. He pushed in another magazine of ammunition and pulled back the slide with ease.

I had never, nor have I since, pitied a human as much as I pitied Benny at that moment, slinking down the hall. I kept Mary's head in close to spare her the sight that I couldn't spare myself. The masked man nonchalantly eased off two more bullets into Benny's chest. I could've told Benny what the end game in his business would be. He may have known himself. And if he had died any other way; anywhere else, I would've said 'Knew it' and felt next to nothing. But watching him hemorrhage every ounce of his blood onto that atrium floor, there was nothing to say. And too much to feel.

The man in the mask walked back towards us. Heather was still against the wall, curled up, when he reached down with his left hand and forcefully raised her to her feet. With the silenced pistol in his right hand, he pointed at me. He moved the gun up and down signally for me to rise. We left the building, and we left five more bodies for black-padded stretchers.

CHAPTER FOURTEEN

I am seldom left scared stiff or speechless. I was both stiff and speechless as the masked man put the three of us into a white van parked in front of my building. The van took off before the sliding door shut. There was a grated partition between the back of the van and the driver. The driver wasn't masked, but I couldn't make out any distinguishing characteristics.

We settled in the back of the van. The man with the gun sat with his back to the partition. The guy's arm never so much as flinched as he fixed the long barrel and silencer at my head. He knew how to handle everything. He was sharp, efficient and fucking scary.

Fifteen minutes into the drive, the driver pulled over. He got out. I heard him tinkering with the license plates and the side of the van. The gunman took his time to speak up.

"This is simple. I talk. You listen. You do what I say, when I say to do it. No questions. No negotiations."

"Wait. You have to let her go first."

Mary was shaking and had my hand clenched firmly in hers.

"No, I don't. Shut up and listen. I want your

computer's hard drive and every piece of paper that has even the remotest link with the Lawson's. I want everything."

I looked at Heather. She wasn't looking anywhere in particular, just away from me.

"Why? The files are--"

"No questions"

"Okay. I'll give you everything I got--"

"Good"

"But my office is a crime scene and there isn't even much there. Leo Lawson paid me to give him everything I had."

Heather looked up in outrage, but said nothing. The gunman went on.

"You gave him copies. Copies of everything you had. I want the originals."

"No, I gave Lawson the originals. The only copies."

"He got copies."

Heather broke her silence.

"Still doing his dirty work. Why don't you just take off the mask? You aren't fooling anyone."

"No, don't take the mask off. We don't know you. Shut up."

I couldn't see the man's facial expression through the mask, but I heard a brief chuckle. It was the first time he wasn't staring at me with his beady green eyes.

"You want the files. Okay. You let my wife go right here and then I'll get them for you."

The silenced pistol and his arm still had not flinched.

"No negotiations."

"You're obviously no one to fuck around with. But you and I know that if those files are really all you want, you aren't going to hesitate for more than a millisecond to kill us as soon as you have them. And as I am looking out for me and mine... If you want the files, you have to make me believe that we're going to get out alive."

"I don't have time for this."

"Make time. She has no fucking idea what's going on. She just got home from another continent. Let her go and I'll stay with you and get you the files."

Mary was holding my arm, but nevertheless she was a fan of my proposed deal. The gunman didn't even consider it.

"I need you alive. I don't need them. I can kill you and your wife and her. And then I can still find your files. But this way, you buy a little time. Where are we going?"

His arm flinched. He moved the gun. He aimed it at Mary.

"Staten Island"

We pulled onto Pierce's road around mid-morning. The driver parked across the street where I had gotten into the cab hours earlier.

"She has the files inside?"

"She should."

"You don't go inside. You don't make any moves. You don't try to signal her or tell her anything. If I get suspicious, they die and then I come after you."

"Yeah. Don't get itchy, asshole. This is a finest and bravest neighborhood."

I bombarded the front door with an arsenal of knocks before backing off the porch. Margie opened the door.

"Where've you been? Pierce called--"

"Get Renee for me."

"Get her yourself."

"Margie, do not fuck with me right now."

"Oh Mr. High and Mighty, do I look like your slave?"

"Please…"

"RENEE!"

Margie stomped off. Renee emerged from the basement. She was still in the same clothes she had on the night before.

"Oh Good. You're alive. I was about to head over to your place."

"What the fuck did you do with the files?"

"What files?"

"The files you were supposed to take over to Lawson."

"I dropped off the copies myself, just like you said, asshole."

"No, I said to drop off the originals. Fuck, Renee."

"You did not say that. We never give originals--"

"Give them to me now."

"They're in my bag."

"Please go get your bag."

"You're such a dick."

Renee headed back down to the basement. I started talking to myself.

"Yeah. I know. And so I drowned. Mass murdering fucks with silenced Sigs kidnapping me, Mary coming home for the day that it starts raining shit, dumb bitches owing the wrong people, fucking drug dealers, pissed off millionaires, pissed off secretaries. I hope Hell treats me better than earth."

I cracked my neck. Renee threw a manila folder at me as she returned.

"Now take me back to your apartment so I can--"

"Fuck no. Stay here."

"Take me back--"

"No. Listen to me. I'm serious. Stay here. Wait to hear and if—if I don't come back for you personally soon, you leave town."

"What is going on now?"

"Don't follow me."

I walked out to the van. Renee went back inside. I slid the van door open. The gunman had his gun squarely pointed at Mary.

"Mary get out."

"The files…"

I threw the folder at his feet and hoped into the van.

"Close the door. Open the envelope and show me."

Only a moment after I had closed the van door, it flew back open.

"You know, Graves, you have a lot of fucking nerve… Aw fuck"

I cracked my neck. Renee stood at the door, a sudden movement away from getting two bullets in her skull. The gunman was still masked and motioned with his gun.

"Get in. Close the door."

I never thought I could honestly empathize or sympathize with desperate men. I always scoffed at them. Who let's themselves get into those kinds of situations? What kind of fucking moron can't see it coming? Can't get out of the way? Make a way out if you can't find one. Fuck your environment. If you come into the world with a brain, may as well use it. I used to be crude. Then I became rude and lewd. But sitting between Mary and Renee in the back of that car, I was just plain desperate.

"You could've warned me."

"The thought occurred to me."

The gunman was on his cell phone and he shushed us. He wasn't speaking. He was listening. This was a very good sign. He was taking orders. That instilled a modicum of optimism in me.

We pulled over again. Before I could do anything, the gunman ripped off his mask. It was Lawson's driver, Gregory. I had given almost no thought to who he was before then. I was so disheartened to see him rip off the mask. He was suddenly certain that he didn't care if we knew who he was. That meant we were all dead already in his eyes.

"Listen closely."

"Look, there are other ways to do this… we can--"

"Shut up. Show some respect."

"For you? You're a coward pointing a gun at three— Okay two innocent women."

He made an abrupt movement towards Mary. I flinched and submitted, saying, "Alright. I won't talk anymore."

"My boss wants to see you."

The driver was a short Hispanic guy, armed and anxious. We switched into an SUV in a parking lot with the Verrazano not far off in the background. The office building was somewhere on the Upper East Side.

"My friend will go with you. You go inside. You talk to the man. They stay here with me. Now, you have to impress him."

The driver walked through the back door of the building. I followed him through the door, down the hall and into the service elevator. He hit the button for the 16th floor. The elevator brought us to an atrium with a secretary's desk and a glass door in front of it. We went through the doors and met the secretary. She looked prim and proper at her perch.

"You can wait in the car. Thank you."

The driver took a second or two to process what the secretary said. I pointed towards the elevator. She pointed towards the hallway for me.

She led me down the hall as the driver went back to wait for the elevator. There were offices all along the hall. Each one had a heavy wooden door and a large glass panel. The offices were empty. Some had a phone inside. Then two offices in a row were filled with boxes for computers, TVs and various electronic sundries.

It struck me as a reasonable investment property for a man like Leo Lawson. There was a full view of the river. It wasn't too removed from Midtown.

The secretary came to a halt at the end of the hall. She held the door open to the last office in the corridor.

Folding chairs were set up throughout the room. A couple of guys were pacing around. One played with his cell phone. There were two crappy tables decorated with food wrappers. There was a large leather sofa against the wall. And there was his chair.

A big black swivel chair sat in the middle of the room. It was the kind of chair they put it on a pedestal at Staples. Like you would for the Holy Grail. In their defense, it was a good-looking chair.

August Summers stood with his back to me talking to one of his henchmen. The henchman was sitting on the couch against the wall. He stood up when he saw me enter. Summers took a quick glance at me. He turned back around to finish his conversation. The henchman nodded and walked past me, out of the room.

"Do you go on a last name basis with everyone? I hear that everyone calls you Graves."

"So you have one working sense. What the fuck are you going to do with my wife and secretary?"

"I heard you were rude too."

"What do you want?"

"I wanted to meet. You've become such an annoyance that I had to put a face to the name. See for myself."

"You're August Summers. I know you and what you're about. And now, you know what I look like."

"You're very impatient. As far as I can make out, you don't have many redeeming qualities."

"I guess we have that in common, but then again I don't peddle illegal substances to the destitute to profit from their misery and addictions."

"You preach too, huh, Graves? I hear you're no saint yourself. You work the world just like the rest of us. It's a business; an industry born out of the true capitalistic nature of humans. Not even laws can keep people from profits."

"Yeah, but maybe Attica or Clinton or wherever the fuck you wind up can."

"Graves, you've been dealing with my nephew, his people, Heather and Leo Lawson. These are ignorant, disreputable... more civil people. They're the kind that goes to jail. But I'm not."

"So you're saying looks are deceiving, huh? What do you--"

As the words left my mouth, the large Hispanic male to my right pummeled the right side of my face. I wasn't sure if it was a good thing that I had gotten pistol-whipped on the other side of my face or if that would've made me a bit more numb for the thumping. I held my hand to the right side of my face. Summers got up out of his chair.

"George, go get a towel from the bathroom, run it under some warm water…"

The boxer walked over to the bathroom. It was attached to the office.

"The bathroom is part of the Luxury Executive Suites. We've only rented out a few floors so far. The perk to that is that there are a lot of open floors. I have plenty of space to spread out. I have all my employees set down on the 7th floor. I keep my other associates entertained up here on the 16th. They like the view."

"I would think they'd get confused with all this glass around. Break their fucking necks walking into windows and shit."

Summers received the towel in one hand and passed it over to me with the other.

"I don't have much love for my old rackets anymore. I've gone legitimate… for the most part. I still have my minor infractions here and there. I charm a lot of city and state officials, contractors and corporate types in shady manners. But for all intents and purposes, I'm legitimate. Let me put it like this: I don't like to spend my time dealing with Rolando or his type of bullshit much anymore."

"Yeah, I can see how signing death warrants could get tiring."

The Hispanic heavy handed associate stepped up. Summers waved him off.

"Stubborn fuck, aren't you? See one of your problems is that you think you know everything. It's not surprising. You were a cop. And the biggest problem with cops is they think they're smarter than everyone. That's because they deal with stupid people, for the most part. It creates this stigma. Cops start thinking because everyone's a suspect, and everyone's a criminal in one way or another, that they must be smarter than everyone. But see only a stupid person would think he's smarter than everyone. And that's what cops really are. They're stupid. Some are semi-intelligent, smarter than the average criminal. But they still aren't the smartest guys in the room. Cops also have the initial leg up. They have more resources at their fingertips and few guys out there know how to commit the perfect crime. So I don't give them a lot of credit because... hey, if they were smart they wouldn't be fucking cops. There's no money in it, no glory, no nothing...I mean what is there? Huh? ...Just a false sense of honor and entitlement... and a lifetime as a loser. You're the perfect example."

"Why's that?"

"If you were smart, you never would've gotten involved in business that wasn't yours to get involved in."

"I suppose you're right. You must be a real a winner. The ingenuity you possess--"

The small smirk that laid across Summers' face departed. I tried to make up ground.

"—is staggering, but you've failed to realize people pay me to get involved in their business."

"That's a terrible shame."

"I don't usually mind."

"You're going to mind today."

I cracked my neck. He got up and walked around for a bit. I decided to incite his proposal.

"I'd be dead, if you wanted that. So why don't you tell me what you do want?"

"Real Estate"

"Real Estate? I rent."

"That's what it's all about. Proprietorship. Owning something. Real Estate. I started just to gather assets. Launder money. Then I flipped a condo fifteen years ago. It was exhilarating. Fucking fascinating, gut-wrenching, unbelievable thrill. I read every Donald Trump book I could get my hands on, got my real estate license, made a firm, got partners, integrated horizontally, vertically. I climbed. I did it all. And today, I sit here a man with a small fortune who owns a share in the skyscraper he's standing in."

"Congratulations."

"I detect a note of sarcasm, but I'll say thank you just the same. You have to understand that in real estate the real money is in the development phase, the ground floor. You want to get in early. You want to get in at the beginning. Get involved in the middle or towards the end, you're likely to get screwed. So recently, I have been investing in properties in the hopes of developing both commercial and residential real estate, mostly in north Jersey but I have a few projects here in the city. For these projects you, naturally, have to arrange for certain raw materials and other sorts of goods and services."

"Naturally"

"See I'm trying to help you out here. And you're missing my fucking point. As a businessman I look for the least costly ways to operate. This is where everything should start coming together for you. I guess you're not smart enough to get it. You could call these guys here on the sixteenth floor my alternative whole sellers. They make people work a whole lot cheaper than the competition and they find good supplies cheap. Rolando knew that's what I'm interested in these days. Now we had fallen out of touch after my sister passed, but I had seen to his needs while he served his sentence. And then he got lucky and got out. But when he got out, I was out of that business and he wasn't right for this business. I think he was trying to win back some affection or show some appreciation, so he came to me a month or two ago with an idea."

"That's dangerous. Him having an idea, that is."

A missile hit the right side of my face with Summers' blessing. I picked myself up, nursing my jaw yet again.

"It's not kind to speak ill of the deceased. Show a little

respect."

"May I respectfully guess the idea had to do with Heather Lawson?"

"Indirectly. Rolando said that he had recently become close with some women who grew up very rich, here in Manhattan. They had rich and influential fathers. Very rich and influential."

"Leo Lawson"

"Rolando figured out he was heavily involved with shipping and the importing of a great deal of raw goods all around the north east. The kind of raw goods used in the development of commercial and residential properties. And sure enough, I was in the market for some goods being imported fairly regularly by some of his ships."

"How convenient"

"Exactly what I said. And when opportunity presents itself as a present ...you open it. He has the ability to tinker with manifests, fool the right people and get me what I need. So I set up a deal with Rolando and Heather with assurances that Leo Lawson was onboard. Unfortunately the communication broke down between the various parties involved and mid deal Heather disappeared with a nearly 500 thousand dollars down payment I made. Naturally, I was upset. I sought out Leo, to settle things and he... blew me off, which is unfortunate. He told me he never signed anything and he wasn't responsible for Heather's malfeasance."

"Okay. So have them killed. That sounds fair to me."

"Graves, I just got through explaining how I've gone legitimate. I have no interest in bodies and blood. Those are expenses. I just want my shit."

"No interest in bodies or blood?"

"No"

"So take back what's yours."

"I don't need to steal anything. I need what's mine and...I don't know where it is. That's what I want you to find out. I want you to make Leo Lawson tell you how I can get what I paid for."

"That's what you want me to do?"

"Yes."

"And if I get him to listen--"

"He will listen to you because you will make him listen to you. I don't give a shit how you do it. I don't like to micromanage. I just want you to do it. I know you two have done business before. I want you to tell him that for all the pain and suffering he has caused me, I have decided that he will not get the other million and a half I promised. I want Leo Lawson's full cooperation and I want everything I asked for. And I want it now. Today. If I don't get what I want...I may have to regress to my old self. Understand?"

"I think so. And you have to understand that I need assurances that my wife and my secretary live."

"We'll deal once you--"

"We'll deal now. I'm dead. Heather's dead. I get that. But the bodies end there. Mary and Renee don't know about you. They don't know anything. They'll be as lost as everybody else when this is all done. They don't need to die."

"Well, I'll talk to Gregory, but if that's true then... Hey, I'm a businessman. I think I can tolerate some profit sharing for this deal. If I get everything I want, without any fuckups or problems, then they can live. You can have my word on that."

"Your word is shit."

"No, Graves. Right now my word is law. That's the God's honest truth. Keep in mind that those women are all as good as dead right now. If I get phone call with the whereabouts of my goods, they're a little less dead. If I get all my goods, they're not dead at all. I'll give you four hours. That's the deal."

"What's Lawson's address?"

"Good. 972 Park, I believe. Give him a burner."

Someone handed me a cell phone.

"Don't bother calling anyone but me. And don't even fucking bother calling until Lawson agrees to send every container."

Two thugs grabbed me. I was sitting on the ground, leaning up against the sofa. I took a second or two to get up. Three associates stood between Summers and me. Summers was staring at me, standing with his arms resting on the back of his chair.

"Oh. And Graves, incase you wanted to turn me in or get the cops to help you, you should know that I'll go willingly. I have a great attorney. I won't worry. I'll get turned loose. But those women will be dead before I turn in a statement. You're wanted for murder. There's APB out for you. You don't want to die in Rikers. So do as your told and keep your head down."

I chuckled as I leaned on the back wall of the elevator. Watching the doors slowly close on me, I cracked my neck. There were a number of things I could've done, but I didn't think of any of them. Instead, I battled to keep my eyes open and aimed myself west, towards Park.

CHAPTER FIFTEEN

Once out on the street, I took off my coat which had various blood stains on it at that point. As my cab pulled over, I heard someone lay on the horn further down the street. It caught my attention and I looked back. The man Summers had sent out of the room as soon as I had arrived was trying to pull out of a spot.

I had been making shit up as I went along and it had not paid off. I was furiously trying to conjure up some plan as I took the short trip to Lawson's. Exiting the cab, the only thought that occurred to me was I deserved death. Summers' man pulled into a spot on a side street a block off, barely in sight. There was a doorman at the desk inside.

"Can I help you?"

"Not really. Lawson in the Penthouse?"

"And who may I say is here?"

"Graves"

"Just...Graves"

I made no effort to respond.

"All right...Mr. Lawson, there is a Mr. ... Graves down here to see you... He says to call his office."

"Oh well this is pretty fucking urgent."

"...Yes...He says it's very urgent. All right, I'll send him up."

He muttered, "6th floor."

I took the elevator to the sixth floor. I knocked. Lawson answered.

"Mr. Graves, I was under the impression that we had concluded all our business."

"Yeah, well, we forgot to take into account a certain businessman."

"What happened to your head?"

"A certain businessman... and his nephew"

"Am I supposed to know who--"

"Summers"

"Come in."

I walked in. Lawson was hesitant to have me in. There was a kid's toy lying underneath a table. It stuck out. A maid quickly emerged and caught me eying it. She grabbed it and walked down a hall. I tweaked my neck and peered down the hall to see her enter a door. She was talking to someone inside the room down the hall,

"No. No. Don't touch that. Here, I found--"

I ignored the maid and the child. Lawson was already halfway to his study.

"I would've thought my 'payoff' concluded your involvement in all this. Did Summers offer you a better deal?"

"I guess you could say he roped me in."

I migrated towards Lawson's small bar. I went right for the decanter whiskey, neglecting to ask. I already had the drink poured when I looked up to see a befuddled leer from Lawson. He shrugged me to go ahead. I drained the glass rather hastily. Lawson began to speak.

"That doesn't seem very wise on your behalf. I've been briefly acquainted with his reputation and history-- Would you like a towel or something for your head and the blood?"

"It's mostly dried blood now. So if you know things

like he's a former drug kingpin who weaseled his way out of two RICO indictments and almost every charge ever brought against him, and that he has had dozens of men murdered in the past twenty years... I have to ask why you would've jumped to bed with him."

"Excuse me. Jumped into bed with?"

"Something about containers off your boats for two million in cash. Sounding any more familiar?"

"It sounds familiar... and ludicrous. I have to apologize. My daughter and her friends have a very naïve view of how this world works."

"An apology isn't going to cover this one. You need to live up to your end of the deal."

"There was never any deal. Heather came to me at her mother's funeral. I welcomed the chance to grieve with what family I have left, but she was more interested in having me partake in some half-brained scam with this Summers. She pestered me for some time and Summers had some of his lackeys come around here and my office. I've had my security tightened and last I spoke to Heather, she was abandoning the scheme."

"She didn't. And now she's in a car with a gun to her head. My wife and secretary are in the same precarious situation. You're going to help me get them un-kidnapped."

I poured another.

"How do I know you aren't lying to me?"

"Do I look like I'm fucking with you?"

"No, you don't."

"Because I'm not."

"Well, shit. We can't do any good. We need to call the police."

"No, I'd at least like to try and get them back alive."

"Oh for God's sake. What can we--"

"You can give him his shit."

"I don't have the faintest idea what he's talking about. Heather said that I would have to make a few containers go missing. That's not child's play at New York ports. Everything is tracked by computers and very closely guarded. There are a lot of interests at stake every second."

"Wait. You're telling me you don't have, nor can you get the containers he wants. Right?"

"That's what I'm telling you."

"We are talking about several peoples lives. Your daughter among them."

"Don't question my love for my daughter. This situation is simply absurd."

"Ha-ha. I'm very well aware of that, Mr. Lawson. Though, it is rather difficult to delicately explain the absurdities to psychopaths. Now, I don't have much time here. Your daughter fucked up and got a lot of people killed. I don't take this lightly, Mr. Lawson. I don't take the possibility of losing two women very close to me... lightly. I think it would behoove both of us to get past the absurd nature of our predicament and move towards a plan of action."

"I don't remember what he wanted... I can get my hands on some cash today, not two million dollars, but maybe enough to buy him off."

"No, cash won't do. It's the principle of it. He feels entitled to this shit. And he most certainly doesn't want to look like he was bested. He's a silly, soulless criminal desperate to be seen as an industrial tycoon. If you can't get him what he wants, then we have to con him into thinking that we're giving him what he wants. ... And hope we escape before he figures it out."

"...And sends us floating down the river."

"...Yeah."

"You're sure about not involving the police?"

"For now... Cops can be inept. Things can get leaked too many ways. I don't want to take the chance. We'll call them when the time's right."

"Have you done something like this before?"

"I don't know. Depends what 'this' is and how you

qualify it. But I don't think so."

"So how do we con him?"

"Misdirection."

"I meant more specifically."

Lawson pulled back the decanter of whiskey. It had taken off the edge but it was a good thing he pulled it away. I needed some wits.

"They say it's never wise to underestimate your enemies."

"They say a lot of bullshit. You overestimate. I'll underestimate. Shit will balance out. We're going to need to show him some containers or a ship or some shit. Something by the docks or somewhere where he'll be bemused by his surroundings, allowing us to slip out while Summers is still smiling."

"Do you really think that will work?"

"It's the only way I can think to play it."

"...I have a place by the yards where I send my company's old, misplaced or mislabeled containers. It's not very big, but I keep a good number of containers there with a manager and a couple of security guards on staff for it."

"Okay. What's the layout like?"

"Well it's right on the water; open, not enclosed by anything but a fence with barb wire. There's a little security booth. Most of the containers are empty. There's a trailer, a couple of fork lifts, nothing too valuable. One gate. That's it."

"Okay. We tell him that his containers are x, y and z but he lets us go first and we call him from the road and tell him which. We get on the road, call the police instead and ride off into the sunset."

"And if he rejects the proposal? Asks to check the containers?"

"I think this plan may be weak enough without you picking away at it."

"My apologies, but it does sound tough to live through

your plan."

"It would be nice if we had a better strategist, greater forces and maybe some guns. But at this point I think we're just going to have to make due and pray that we get lucky. He wants a clean business deal. We'll make him think he's got one."

Lawson looked hesitant, but willing. I thought it'd be a miracle if he actually went along with my so-called 'plan'. I couldn't think of any way that it wouldn't end bloody. We we're all too expensive alive. I could only slightly justify recruiting and luring Lawson to what I assumed was his death. The direness made him too amenable for his own good.

"My driver and bodyguard, Gregory was Special Forces. He may be helpful."

"No, I think he's done enough. He's got a new job with Summers."

"No"

"Oh yes. You employed quite the guy."

"Christ, this is all so hard to believe."

"You should get on the phone with the manager at your depot or whatever and tell him and the rest of the employees to take the rest of the day off."

"Alright, anything else?"

"Just the call"

"... Oh! Do you think we should be armed?"

The antique cabinet stretched from floor to ceiling in a room that, I assume, doubled as his wife's closet. It had multiple large glass panels and a few smaller cupboards at the foot of the cabinet. Red velvet lined the inside. Perfectly and meticulously spaced out on the velvet-lined interior of the large cabinet were nearly a dozen guns. There were two rifles, over a half dozen pistols and a musket.

"Is that a musket?"

"I'm not sure. I don't like guns."

"Ha-ha. I can tell."

"No, they...were my wife's. She liked to shoot. She believed that they were a necessary evil. That it was our responsibility to protect ourselves."

"Survival of the armed"

I pulled back the hammer on a 38 and squeezed the trigger. The click from the hammer hitting the empty chamber rang out.

Lawson got on the phone and called his depot manager. The security guards and manager agreed to leave for the day. I grabbed three of the pistols from the case. With my hands full, I asked Lawson, "Do you have a gym bag or something to carry these in?"

"I think I can find something."

"And do you have any antiseptic, things to clean up my head with?"

"The bathroom is over there. Check the bottom drawers."

"Thanks."

Lawson left for his bedroom. I headed for the bathroom. I dabbed my wounds with some rubbing alcohol, moaned and shabbily cleaned the cuts. I tried to run my head under the faucet but it was impossible so I ended up throwing handfuls of water over my head. My head was throbbing and I found myself continually cracking my neck, groaning at my stream of dismal thoughts. I remember looking at my haggard self in the mirror, wishing I could fast forward through the next few days and at the same time, knowing I couldn't trust any other human to do what I had to do. I rubbed my jaw and examined it more closely in the mirror.

There was a moment where I caught my eyes in the mirror. I didn't see what I needed. I remember feeling like my back was giving out. I crumpled over the sink. I had all my weight on it. I remember thinking it should buckle, but it didn't.

I recovered slowly, buttoned my shirt and went back to the gun case. Lawson had disappeared. I focused on retrieving the necessary items from the case.

Lawson returned with a pistol in one hand and a gym bag in the other. He handed the gun to me butt first. I won't lie. It was a relief. When I first spotted him with the gun, I expected a bullet and an end to the charade.

"She kept one in the bed side table."

He pulled a stack of hundreds out of the bag. He held it out.

"What's that for?"

"An incentive... for Heather's safety and my own."

"Put it back in your bedside table."

The two of us sat at either side of the table in his study loading magazines with ammunition.

"What about these?"

"No. Those are for the 38. I already loaded that. That's the revolver. Just leave the box in the bag."

"Less efficient weapon in a gunfight"

"Yeah"

"I warn you I won't be a crack shot if that is what it comes down to."

"Neither will I. We'll be firing bullshit not bullets. These are just safety precautions."

Lawson was unconvinced. I handed him a Beretta butt first.

"Here. Don't shoot yourself, but keep this on you. They won't expect you to be carrying one. They're never comfortable to carry but make sure the safety is down and ...uh...tucking it in the back of your pants or between your belt and your pants is the best way to do it."

"And to shoot?"

I released the clip and demonstrated how to cock back the slide.

"That puts one in the barrel when the clip is in. This is the safety... On... Off. When you want to shoot put it in the off position. You won't see the red dot. Line up the sights. Aim for center mass. Squeeze."

"Simple enough."

"Yeah. I wish it wasn't. Don't load the chamber until later."

"All right."

"Do you have a car we could use apposed to a taxi or... the subway?"

"I keep a few in a garage around the corner."

"Great. ...Your wife didn't keep any bullet proof vests, did she?"

"No."

"Just asking"

Lawson nodded slowly. He walked off sullenly. I organized the guns. The bag was full of ammo and heavy metal weapons that clinked against each other. I took a 380 Sig, slammed in the clip, pulled back the slide, released a bullet into the chamber, made sure safety was on and snuggly fit it into my pants. I waited near the door to the apartment. I watched Lawson exit the room that I had watched the housekeeper enter earlier. The housekeeper stood in the doorway. He said a few words to her then left her at the door.

"Never have a housekeeper that has kids."

"I'll make a note of that."

He opened the door towards the small atrium and the elevator.

"Does the building have a back door?"

"There's a side entrance."

"Okay. I'm going to need your housekeeper for a minute and... duct tape, if you have it."

The street had parked cars and various structures to mask my not-so-sly trek out the side entrance to position myself. I carefully staged myself on the corner just out of Summers' man's sightlines.

The housekeeper exited the front of the apartment building and headed in my direction. She walked past me and moved towards the tails' vehicle. I pulled out the 380. I did my best to conceal it in public but I needed it in hand. The housekeeper wrapped on his window. I sprung.

He was telling her to go away through the window when I pulled the back door open. I had the gun snuggly wedged in the goon's neck before he could fully turn around.

"Roll up the window. Both hands on the wheel."

"What the fuck are you doing?"

"Shut up. Put the car in drive, pull out and pick up the lonely old man up there with the black gym bag."

I pushed the gun into the back of his head. He did what I said. Lawson entered and sat in the passenger seat.

"Lawson, pat him down. See if he's got a cell phone and check if he's got a gun under his seat."

Lawson did as I asked. But the mope pulled his hands down off the wheel. I batted the barrel of the gun into the back of his head.

"Hands on the fucking wheel"

"Alright. Alright. I'm only here to make sure things go smoothly."

"Well, they won't. So you're useless."

Lawson pulled a cell phone out of the man's pocket.

"I don't think he's got a gun under his seat."

The driver insisted, "Why would I have a gun? This is a simple business--"

"Check the glove box."

Lawson found a 45 and passed it back with the cell phone.

"Look, your squirt gun."

"I didn't know that was in there. It's my buddy's car."

"Yeah. Do me a favor and refrain from talking. Take a left at the light."

"Mr. Lawson, you should rethink this. He's a businessman--"

"Shut up. Ha-ha. What'd he do? Brainwash you with a brochure."

"I am happy 'bout where I am. Better than being you."

Lawson seemed indifferent and hadn't made eye contact with the driver. He made eye contact as he spoke to him for the first time.

"Didn't my friend tell you to shut the fuck up?"

The driver huffed. He pulled in to the parking garage.

"Lawson, tell the attendant we want to park ourselves. He won't like it. So demand it."

Lawson got out spoke to the attendant. We plunged down into the depths of the garage. I made him park in an empty corner.

"This is a stupid move. Do you really think you and the old man are going to get away with this? He'll just kill them and then come after you."

"Would you shut up? You're a fucking henchman. Nobody wants your forecast."

I knocked him over the head with my piece. It didn't knock him out but he was dazed and easier to handle. Lawson waited outside the car as I finished subduing the little shit. I mangled him with two full roles of duct taped. I used the seatbelt, seat and steering wheel to make sure he was properly incarcerated with no hope of escape. It looked comical, but so was he.

"It ain't pretty, but we don't want him talking to Summers before we do."

"He looks subdued."

We began to walk up.

"...Ya know it fucking pisses me off that they don't get it, these fucking punks. They're the same. None of them have any distinguishing attributes. They're in a rigged game and they don't get that. How badly has the world failed them? One goes out, one comes in. It's cops and robbers. It's a seriously ironic and tragic game of cops and robbers, but that's what it is. A fucking game. A game that nobody wins. Cops lose less, but there are no winners. Punks like that are luckier than a fucking leprechaun if they get out of the game while they've still got two legs and a dick in-between 'em. Cops own the game board. They rig the game because they know they can't actually win anything, because when you bust one, another one comes in. And all of 'em keep playing, thinking it's just too much fucking work to change the game. Policing these days just means keeping the perpetual bullshit cycling. Cops don't get it. Corner kids don't get it. Everybody thinks that they're going to be the one that gets what they want. Nobody gets it. Nobody wins."

Lawson looked intrigued as I spouted out the facts of life. I'm not sure if he was intrigued by what I said or the fact that I said it. Either way, I told him something.

CHAPTER SIXTEEN

The attendant handed Lawson a set of keys. Lawson tipped him generously. We walked over to a Porsche SUV parked in an expensively accessible spot.

"The trick is to always tip them. Then they keep it right up front. Would you drive?"

"Sure"

I placed the bag in the back seat. I tinkered with the seat and started the car.

"It's a good thing I wore my contacts. I warn you, Mr. Lawson, I haven't driven a car in a very long time."

"I assure you, my boy, I haven't driven in a great deal longer."

We drove in silence for some time. He was staring out the window when he asked, "How long have you and your wife been married?"

"Ah. We were married about-- It was six years in May."

"Bit late in life to find love."

"Well, I was... I tend to look in the wrong places."

"Does that imply current marital issues?"

"Yeah. She left me two years ago and arrived out of the blue today... out of all the days she could've."

"At least she's back. Do you still love her?"

"I love everybody."

Lawson wasn't enthused by my answer. He started to look away again so I gave him a better response.

"I don't know how to be sure about loving her. I can read the signs different ways."

"Love is never that elusive. It's there or it isn't. There doesn't need to be any signage. My wife used to yell from the bed for me to bring her the paper. I would be in my study. She would be in bed; closer to the door, and the paper. And yet every Sunday morning she would yell for the times. Her beckoning for the Sunday Times started every argument I can remember. I resented her then, but I still loved her. In hindsight, those could've been our greatest moments. I should've relished the chance to bring her the paper in bed."

It was difficult to listen to the man lament, so torn by grief. His stories and gloomy demeanor only made my anxiety and uncertainties accumulate.

"Get off here, then it's a left and you follow the road down to the water."

It was silent. I felt compelled to come up with something to say. Then in as incurious of a fashion as I could, I asked, "Oh. Not that it matters much at this point, but for my own edification, ya know... Where is Michael?"

"What?"

"That was the job originally. To find him."

"I didn't lie. He's in Japan; returning home this week."

"Why not just tell Heather that?"

"I spoke to her for the first time in five years, and look where it got me. I want him as far from Heather and Samantha as possible."

"So why bring him--"

"This is it."

I pulled up to a gate. Lawson exited. He unlocked the gate and pulled it back. I pulled the car forward. There was a security booth to the left. It was empty as requested. There were two truck cabs and some machinery parked next to each other in the back corner of the gated depot. In front of the cabs was the trailer, which I imagined housed the office for the depot manager. I turned the car around, positioning it to face the gate and in prime position for a quick getaway.

The containers were arranged in long columns. There were six or seven rows. The containers were equally spaced out within the gated limits of the facility. There were about six feet in between containers. There were a few sets of containers that were vertically stacked near the far end. In all there were more than a hundred containers but no more than a hundred and fifty. The containers were different colors. Some looked older and rusted. It wasn't what I imagined but it wasn't as if I was making any choices.

It was a scary metal maze.

"So this is it. Most of the containers are empty. The boxes up front will either be moved to a ship or wherever they're supposed to be. Everything gets moved around. It isn't much. I have other--"

"It'll do. It's a good place for a showdown."

"Are you thinking of this as the...Okay Corral?"

"Nah.

I pulled out the phone Summers had given to me. I found the only number in the phone book. I dialed it. Someone picked up.

"Yes"

"It's Graves."

There was a short pause.

"Where are you?"

"I'm standing next to containers full of industrial goods for your entrepreneurial endeavors and waiting for the sunset."

"Where exactly? Give me the address."

"Now, Summers, you should realize how this works. You drop the girls off at some public place, they call me and tell me--"

"It works like this. You tell me the address and I may or may not arrive with your women. And if you don't, I kill one every ten minutes until my dinner reservations. Get me?"

"Get this, you inbred ass clown. You keep making threats and you ain't getting shit."

"I'll bring the women. They can go as soon as I see my containers. What is the address?"

"...188 Liberty, Brooklyn. It's an outdoor container depot on--"

"I'll find it."

I hung up. I threw the phone into a pocket. Lawson's skepticism had become second nature to me at that point. His facial expressions were wildly dubious and dripping with concern. All I needed was for him to stand around a little longer. I pulled out my cell phone and dialed Pierce. I grabbed the bag of guns I surveyed the yard searching for a place to stash them.

"Pierce"

"Graves. Holy Shit"

"I know. I'm in deep shit. Look, I need you to do something."

"You need to come in right now."

"Later. For now, do this for me."

"What?"

"Call Hope. Tell him to get ESU ready to hop to it on my say so. I've got Summers arriving with 3 hostages and he's already admitted to me he's responsible for killing Rolando, Benny, Hal, Ron, all of them. They should be here within half an hour."

"Where are you?"

"Leo Lawson and I are waiting for him."

"Where?"

"You can't move right away. He's got Renee and Mary."

"What?"

"Alright. Look, it's 188 Liberty, Brooklyn. It's on the

water. You can't give Hope the address until I say so. We have to do it my way. I can't let anyone fuck this up."

"Are you intent on fucking with me right now, Graves. Come on."

"Make the call to Hope. Just make the call, Pierce."

"And say what? Ready the forces for D-Day, but I can't tell you where Normandy is?"

"Something like that"

"Fuck, Graves. Don't do this--"

"I will call this number when I want you to move in, transfer it to Hope so he can barge in then--"

"I'll try."

I put the phone away. Surveying the arena, I said to Lawson, "Wyatt Earp made it out of the Okay Corral alive, right?"

"He did. I'm not sure about everyone else."

We reentered the car and waited. Half an hour later two black Cadillac's pulled around the corner in the distance. I hit send on my phone, and put it on speaker.

"Pierce"

"Yeah. I got Hope and the ESU Sergeant ready."

"They're here. I'm leaving the phone on speaker in my pocket."

I carefully slid the cell phone into my jacket. I exited the car. I left both doors open on the driver's side and the car running. Lawson exited without looking to me for approval. He handed me a piece of paper.

"I chose random containers from the first few rows and wrote down the numbers."

"Right. The guns are on the other side of the third row."

"I remember."

"If you get chance, get the women in the car and drive."

The black Cadillac's parked side by side in front of the manager's trailer. The SUV parked closer to the trailer and the sedan a few feet to its left. The windows were tinted. I couldn't tell who was in which car.

The back window of the sedan shrank into the door. One of Summers' right hand men was sitting in the closest seat. Approaching the car, I noticed Summers sitting on the other side of him. Summers spoke first.

"Which ones are mine?"

"The women?"

"No"

"Get the fuck out of your car. And have your lackeys let the girls out."

I walked back towards Lawson as Summers continued to yell at me. In a huff, Summers got out of his car.

"Don't walk away from me, motherfucker."

"I held up my end of the deal. If you're such an upstanding businessman, why don't you do the same?"

"Get them out of the fucking car."

The front door of the SUV opened. The driver of the SUV opened the back door and the three women piled out. Gregory exited behind them. He still held them at gunpoint. Another man came out of the passenger door of the SUV. With the exodus beginning, the three men from Summers' sedan exited. Facing the petit army from 20 feet back, I began to squirm at the feasible, messy outcomes. I prayed he would civilly hand over the women and the five of us would briskly drive off leaving a dumbfounded Summers to be found by Hope and a not-so-petit army of Emergency Services Unit officers.

As expected and to my dismay, that didn't happen. Summers kicked out the back of Mary's knees as she stood lined up with the other women between the vehicles. He reached back to Gregory for the silenced gun. Mary scrambled away on her knees. She was stopped and raised by a thug by the end of the car. Summers shrugged off her mini-escape and instead grabbed Renee by the hair. Renee screeched. Tears trickled down the side of her face. Amidst everything Heather seemed detached and ambivalent, dead already. I was screaming at Summers during the entire escapade.

"What the fuck! Summers! We had a deal. Me for the women."

"Ah I'll start with her instead. It doesn't make any difference. Right Graves...Right!"

"Hey! Hey! Fuck You! I did what you said. You're here. Look around asshole."

"I don't fucking believe you."

He pushed Renee's head an arms length away and pressed the silencer to the back of her head. Mary and Renee screamed. I did too. Heather froze. Leo was fidgeting, perplexed. Leo quietly asked, "What's going on here?"

"Stay back there. Just hold on. Summers stop! Everybody calm down!"

"Graves, where is--"

"Just hold on."

Summers raised his voice again. He didn't like the idea of me issuing any orders whatsoever.

"Do you think I'm that fucking stupid, Graves? Are you that stupid? ARE YOU?"

"Wait. Stop. Stop. No, I don't. Hey, put down the gun. Just put it down. Here. Here."

I took a step forward. I wrestled around my coat pocket. I accidentally wrestled my phone out of the pocket and it fell behind me. Unfortunately, I didn't notice in all the commotion. I noticed later. I brought out the white piece of paper.

"Here...The container numbers for all the containers you want. You just have to let them go. Everyone walks away happy. A perfect business transaction."

"Give it to me now."

"Come on. Blood's a big expense, right? Let them go."

"NO!"

"I'll stay. You and me, that's what you really want right, huh? ...I'll stay. They all leave. Then I give you the container numbers. Shit, I'll haul some of the containers down to your fucking warehouse. You just got to let them leave. Or I could eat the list..."

Summers thought it over. I was seriously threatening to eat the paper. He wasn't able to put his brain into overdrive with out extenuating his rage. Summers whispered something to Gregory. I assume it was something along the lines of 'Kill them as soon as he hands over the list'.

"It's just good business."

"You stay..."

"Yeah. I stay."

He let go of Renee's hair. He handed the gun back to Gregory. Mary embraced her. Summers grabbed the list from me. The thugs parted ways. The women ran over. Mary headed for the drivers side door. Heather was in the back seat of the car before I blinked. Renee ran towards me.

"Renee, stop. Get in the car. Now. Go. Drive."

"Graves, I'll stay with you."

"Drive-the-fuck-away"

Reluctantly, she ran over to the car. Mary was by the driver's door. She barely gave me a second glance. Only Lawson remained. His uneasiness had passed. He turned caustic, abrasive. I was taken aback.

"What? Leo, go!"

"What is this? You fucking played me?"

"What are you talking about? Get the fuck out of here while you can."

Summers spoke up.

"I'm so glad you could join us, Leo. You don't mind if I call you Leo do you? I just feel that at this point after all we've been through, we could be amicable."

"You all can call me, Mr. Lawson. And all of you can go to hell. Especially you!"

Leo pointed at me with his long shrewd finger.

"You manipulative, shameless bastard. I should have known never to trust you."

"What are you talking about? What are you doing?"

"I knew I was dealing with parasites."

Summers pointed his finger at Lawson.

"You're acting quite rude. I would advise you not to act like that dumb motherfucker to your left and to think before you speak."

"All of you disgust me. You're scum. All of you are. You have no idea--"

"I'm scum. I'm scum! I wanted to be professional. I didn't want to bring it to this. I didn't want to have to fucking kill people. I wanted it to do honest business. But you had to--"

"Your business is drugs."

"Please. I'm a capitalist. My business is wherever the money is."

Summers was getting pissed. Lawson was steaming. I was nervous. I motioned for Mary to leave. I mouthed: "Go"

Mary didn't have to be told twice. The thugs spread out. Two were walking down towards the Porsche. The motor bellowed, startling everyone. In less than a second, she accelerated towards the exit and was almost clear. The thugs looked to Summer. With Summers' approval, Gregory started shooting. Gregory was the only one that got off any rounds. He hit the back window and a tire. But the car got out. I watched it screech around the first corner and move out of sight.

"This would be a good time for ESU. Please tell me you're already moving in."

My phone was lying on the ground feet behind me. Summers was getting more and more furious.

"What the fuck am I paying you for? All of you, what the fuck are you doing?? I said let them get to the car but don't fucking let them leave. What the fuck is wrong with you faggotty ass motherfuckers. God fucking damn it."

Lawson was getting more and more furious.

"You bastards. You scum. I should've stayed with

Michael."

He was engulfed with rage. The thugs were all trying to remove the pistols from their pants or going back to the cars to retrieve them. I moved towards Lawson in an attempt to knock some sense in to him but it was too late.

"Leo! Leo, stop."

Leo was nearing the road. Gregory was taking his time reloading his gun. The various thugs were either holding their guns by their sides awaiting orders from Summers or aiming at me. I had my hands up in the air. They were ignoring Lawson for the most part. Summers was screaming.

"Old man, move another inch and I will fucking kill you. Stop moving! Graves don't fucking move!"

I froze. Time froze. Every second was an eternity. I wanted to be invisible. I wanted to be rescued alive, not found dead. And just when I got through thinking time was going by too slow, it sped up. In a matter of seconds, a nerve was struck and the threshold reached.

Leo was mumbling as he came closer to the road. He stared at me for a few moments with hatred bottled in his eyes. He wasn't moving quickly. Gregory had reloaded his gun and was encroaching. Two other thugs were near his side. It was as Gregory grinned at Lawson that Lawson finally made full eye contact with Gregory. In that split second, Lawson exploded.

"I trusted you too."

Lawson pulled out the pistol from the back of his pants. He did it more efficiently and faster than anyone expected, including Gregory. The professionally trained soldier didn't even have time to get off a round in self-defense before Leo had squeezed off two.

The first bullet missed but the second hit one of the thugs by Gregory's side in the shoulder. Gregory reacted as quickly as you would expect a professional soldier to react in that type of situation. Leo didn't have the chance to squeeze off a third round.

Gregory hit him with two consecutive shots in the chest. Leo fell quickly. I didn't hear him squirm or squeal or expel a final breath. I didn't listen for it either. He fell to the ground like a bag of bricks. Afterwards, Gregory squeezed off a final round into his head for safety's sake.

Leo died on the curb. He got the execution I deserved. I got an opportunity.

As the gunfire to my right ensued, the guns once aimed at me migrated to aim at Lawson. I didn't hesitate. I pulled the 380 from my pants. I jerked down the safety, started to run, and fired towards popular vicinity.

I got six or seven rounds off as I back peddled to the containers for cover. One of the guys went down quickly, within the first few shots. Another went for cover behind the car with Summers and shot off a couple of rounds nowhere near my general vicinity. I saw my phone on the ground. I yelled, "Fuck!"

I fired another shot or two using the container as cover before I started running. I could hear Summers in the background, yelling, "Bad move, Graves!"

Sprinting, I rounded the corner of the container and made it to where I had stashed the bag of guns. Shots rang out and I heard numerous bounce off different containers. All the idiots were yelling at each other, ordering each other around, and I couldn't make out much of what they were saying over my own exasperated breathes. Then there was silence and I heard Summers scream, "Stop fucking around. Get in there and bring me back his fucking head!"

I didn't try and mount a heroic stand and fight half a dozen men. Even if they were morons who had trouble operating the trigger of a gun, let alone aiming one, I didn't want to face them straight up. I had no qualms with running.

I hoped I could lose them in the stacks or find better cover towards the back of the depot. But most of all I hoped I could find a whole in the fence or a back gate out.

I could hear the echoing orders and bickering, but I

wasn't paying attention. I was running. I was also reloading my 380 with another clip from the bag. The bag was heavy and I was definitely out of shape. I ducked behind the end of a container whenever I heard footsteps or voices in the aisle.

It sounded as if Gregory and another guy were nearby. Summers and a man or two were lingering near the containers closer to the cars.

I was recovering behind a container. I popped my head out to look down one aisle, which I intended to then run down. I popped my head out a second time and as I moved into the opening, a goon appeared sixty feet down the aisle. I fired four shots. I hit him twice in the legs and maybe once in the upper body. He wasn't dead but he was on his way.

I ran up to him, still looking for his partners, with my gun extended. I kicked his gun away. He looked at me to say, "Fuck. I'm shot." I told him to shut up.

Gregory came out of nowhere and fired two shots. One missed. The other went through my suit coat and shirt, grazing my torso. I fired back, cursed and ran away. The thug was yelling for Gregory to help as Gregory tried to ask him where I ran. The thug kept asking for help and I heard Gregory shoot him. Then he started running back down the aisle towards me.

He caught up as I slipped. My gun fell out of my hands and was visible in the aisle. Even as I tumbled, I kept moving forward. He missed with two more shots. I rounded the corner of a container, still on my knees. Gregory began to gloat.

"I'll make it quick for you and your women. That's more than you deserve."

He rounded the corner expecting to see me. I had left my gun in sight, and my left shoe had fallen off. It was a nasty spill. I'm not surprised he expected me to still be crawling between containers. In fact, I counted on that.

I had gotten to my feet and back tracked. I grabbed a

nine-millimeter, dropped the bag and sprinted. I circled back around as fast as I could. I came around the last corner wide with the gun steady in hand. Gregory was twenty feet down trying to figure which way I had gone. I aimed quickly. He heard me, but couldn't turn. I fired three times. I hit him twice. He fell once.

I hustled to his body. I only peeked at him briefly before I picked up his gun, the 380 and the bag of guns around the corner. I scanned the area awaiting the next thug to pop out. I wedged my foot back into my shoe. I should've kept running right away, but I just had to have the last words he'd hear.

"You deserve the hurt."

Shots rang out again. They bounced off the container in front of me. I shot back and started running again.

"Fuck. Fuck. Fuck. Fuck. Where are the fucking cops?"

Summers came to his senses and suddenly began looking to escape. The drivers of the two cars must have kept the keys in their pockets because he couldn't start either car. Both drivers were somewhere between crates chasing after me. I heard him yelling,

"Where are the fucking keys? Who has the fucking keys?"

That's when he entered the metallic maze to find the keys to one of the cars. I kept running, cursing the generalized body that was my former employer. I zigzagged through the last rows of crates. I knew that there were probably two guys still mulling around the stacks looking for me. Finally, I reached the end of the depot and the fence. It was solid and inescapable.

I was hyperventilating, clutching the chain-linked fence. I moved back and put my body weight against the end of one of the containers. My gun was drawn, pressed against my rapidly beating heart. Every few seconds, I would hear something and spin my head to the right or left.

I checked the aisle to my left and made the decision to run for the farthest corner. I was near the street then but still at the opposite end in comparison to the manager's trailer, security post and entrance of the fucking rat maze.

My thoughts scattered. My breathing began to regulate and I sounded less like a dying walrus. I decided I couldn't waste any more time. I peered to the right; down the long column with the fence bordering the street. I looked back to my left to make sure I was clear.

I moved down to the first container, peeked into the first perpendicular gap and bolted to the next container. I checked down the next gap, saw nothing and bolted again. By the third repetition of this, I said, "Fuck it."

I attempted to bolt the entire length of the depot without stopping to check each time. I figured they wouldn't have time to react even if they saw me, but I still held my gun in my left hand. Just incase.

Half way to the exit, a shot went through the fence behind me and hit a building on the other side. I ducked into the next gap and looked back to see if the guy had followed me. He hadn't. He appeared a split second later. He was running parallel to my path and hadn't stopped when he first passed me halted in the gap. He was stunned when he saw me. The guy probably expected me to keep running. He was yelling, "He's going for the exit--" as I popped off two rounds.

He fell back against a green container. The blood from the exit wounds smeared against the metal as he slid down the container.

I really wanted the police to be there. I really wanted my phone. I really wanted 911 and a shit load of sirens. I got up before I could think about the men amassing by the entrance. I was near the security booth, fifteen feet from Leo Lawson's bloodied corpse.

I paced around the security booth. I looked inside to see a phone. There was one inside. I surveyed the area around the cars and the trailer. No one was visible. I moved to open the door of the booth when I heard a car door slam shut.

The guy moved out from behind the SUV. I crept backwards. I recognized the guy as the van driver from the second kidnapping stage of my nightmare. Then the sweet music emerged: sirens.

"What a response time."

The driver vanished into the stacks, yelling frantically, "Yo! Mr. Summers. Five O. Police. We got to go."

I began to smile. The squad cars were rounding the corner seven or eight blocks out and I began to smile wider. There had never been a sweeter sound or sight. I walked out confidently. I was certain that with the cops in plain view, Summers would whine and cry and bitch his way into the back of a squad car. I also assumed he was unarmed. I underestimated his demeanor and arms. It was unwise.

I pulled the heavy bag off my shoulder and held it at my side. My gun fell to my side. I was basking in the impending arrival of my ex-comrades. I was so relieved at the sight of them that I prematurely exited my clandestine location.

The goon came out the stacks first.

"Oh shit! Graves is over here."

I got my gun up and on him before he could react.

"It's over. Put your hands up and you might not get shot."

I pointed at the arriving forces. The goon huffed and dropped his gun. He walked towards me with his hands in the air. He moved slowly. He had no intention of being shot for Summers. Who could blame him? The goon stood fifteen feet behind me.

Then Summers emerged.

"Why the fuck do you have your hands up? You fucking pussy."

He shot the goon. He was ten feet away from me when he hit the ground. I barely heard the shots over the sirens. But I managed to sprint ten feet towards the cars. I jumped between the sedan and the Escalade. Summers kept shooting.

"Graves! Look what you did."

His shots were a bit wild. He fired six or seven. The windows shattered. The tires flattened. The metal was punctured. I was being shot at, and I was not happy about it.

In my dive to obtain cover I had dropped my bag five feet behind the car. I finished off the clip firing back at him. I checked to see that it was empty. I cracked my neck. The only ammo left was in that bag. The only loaded gun was the thirty-eight at the bottom of the bag.

"You dumb fuck, they're a block away."

"And I'm right here, motherfucker."

He fired two more bullets as he walked towards me. I was fucked. He was yelling, "You fucked everything up!"

A ricochet hit the window of the SUV and some glass dumped at my feet. He moved closer. The bag, my only defense, was five feet away. It was five feet away and right in plain view and aim for Summers. I knew I needed the bag. I had to have it. It was the only way. The cops were still a block out. Summers was moving quickly. He went for the gun off the goon he had just killed.

I rose as fast as I could. I got to the bag as fast as I could. I barely had a hold of it when I turned to get back behind the rear tire of the sedan. Summers peppered me with bullets but missed on every occasion. I was getting the gun out of the bag as fast as I could when Summers appeared ten feet away, turning to face me between the two cars. He had moved faster than I expected. I was unprepared.

When these things happen, they happen faster then you can believe and faster than you remember. The truth is I'm not sure how fast it happened or what I was thinking. I wasn't thinking I was going to die or 'Oh Shit! That's Summers.'. I wasn't thinking. At that moment, it was instinct taking over; self preservation at its finest. It was survival of the best armed, and it had nothing to do with guns.

I remember I had the bag on my lap. And the bullets went through the nylon at one end of the bag, leaving a sizable rift.

Summers didn't fall quickly. He fell suddenly. There was a whole in the car about five inches from my head. His bullet had barely missed. Smoke was rising out of the barrel of his gun. I could smell it. The gun fell out of his hands. Then, he fell.

It took me a long time to exhale. When I did, I moved my right hand over my chest and arms. I scowled over them to see if I had been hit. I was so sure I had been. But I was intact, no holes that weren't there when I was born. Summers, on the other hand, had two new holes.

One shot hit him near the heart. I was told later it nicked his aorta, which is apparently pretty key if a man wants his heart to keep ticking. The other hit his arm. He didn't die suddenly. It took some time. But the cops were rushing past the gate at that point. The sirens rung loud, but the cops yelled louder. I dropped my gun and had my hands in the air.

My hands were still raised but I moved a few feet over to where Summers was trying to crawl towards the SUV and the gun that had fallen out of his hand.

"I just wanted to stay in business."

I kicked the gun away from him even though it was already too far for him to reach. I looked into his desperate, piercing eyes and continued, only saying, "Yeah".

The cops rushed me from behind and threw up against the SUV. I heard them call for paramedics. There was no point. I watched his eyes. He had been panting furiously and trying to move at first. As a cop encroached with cuffs, Summers' breathing shallowed and he stopped trying to move. I saw the desperation and fear in the whites of his eyes replaced with a glossy emptiness when his chest stopped moving.

The cop arresting me was overzealous about putting me in cuffs. I told him, "You don't need the cuffs."

"The fuck I don't. You got about ten cops who witnessed you shoot a guy."

"C'mon. That was self-defense, and he was an asshole. You should've seen that from a block away."

"Ha-ha. Yeah. Save it for the D.A. The cuffs stay on."

"He's the one that wanted the bloody ending."

I cracked my neck and let the cop push me towards the squad cars.

CHAPTER SEVENTEEN

I had my head propped against the edge of the backseat. Either the squad car or I smelled totally foul. There were patrolman, crime scene unit guys, and heavy armored emergency service unit officers all around. The lights were still flashing on a few cars. The sun had set. Eventually, an irritated Detective Dante Hope stormed up to the car.

"Christ almighty, Graves. You cannot do a single thing the easy way."

"They shot first. I used the force I deemed necessary to preserve what pieces of a life I have left. Self defense."

"Oh I see. So you didn't plan this whole thing out? Including the bag full of handguns and the bodies?"

"...No. My intention was to amicably resolve our differences."

"Graves, don't talk. You're only going to get yourself into deeper shit."

"It gets deeper?"

"Yeah. Think an abyss."

He started to shut the door on me.

"Wait! Wait!"

"What?"

"What about the women? They're okay."

"More or less. That's an entirely different pile of shit."

"What do you mean?"

"They're alive and fine. They crashed three blocks down, after they came around the corner. They held up the whole fucking first wave of blue and whites. The Lawson girl bolted but the other two are getting checked out at the hospital. If you don't catch 'em at the hospital, you'll see 'em at the precinct."

"But they're okay?"

"As far as I have been informed, they are in spectacular condition--"

The Medical Examiner's team was wheeling two black bags on stretchers past the car as Hope finished his sentence.

"Which I cannot say for these poor fucking corpses... Or you."

"Are they going to try to charge me?"

"I should hope so. With all the fucking trouble you put my ass through, the least these fucks can do is charge you with something. Summers or any of the rest... didn't happen to cop to icing all my D.O.A.s, did they?"

"Not in so many words. But if I were you I would be very interested in looking at the ballistics reports on the guns found here and at my apartment."

"Yeah. One dead in an alley, three dead in your office, five dead at your place, seven dead here and you..."

"Yeah. There's a body down in the village too. Charles Street. A girl in a bath tub missing most of her head, probably Sam Carlson, Lawson's roommate. Somebody has probably called it in by now, but anyway it's another body. And tell them to look at Heather Lawson for that."

Hope looked over me as I fidgeted and moaned. He gave a quick chuckle looking me over.

"You are unbelievable. All this blood and all these bodies and you, without a one fucking scratch."

"No. See I got one. I got grazed. It went right through my shirt. I even got some butterflies on it before they threw me back here. I got pistol whipped too, but that was earlier... Guess I'm just smarter than the average bear."

"I'm sure you think so."

"Why else do you think I keep outliving 'em?"

"You ain't average. I will give you that. You ain't average. I'd save what energy you have left for the impending inquisition, Yogi."

Hope slammed the door. He approached the grouping of detectives outside the car. He must have told them to guard me at the hospital and get me to the house right after. A patrolman got in the car and drove me away. I looked out the window as we passed Lawson's wrecked Cayenne. The hood was crushed. The airbags were visible. A tow truck was pulling it away from a telephone pole and back on to the street.

I was so tired once they threw me into the interrogation room that they could've gotten me to say anything if they promised I would get to go to sleep after. My head was resting against my shoulder. My eyes were shut. I cracked my neck and my head bobbed back and forth. I was almost asleep when Hope and two other detectives walked in.

"Wake up, Graves"

"You sure I need to be awake for this?"

"Fitzgerald and Finch"

The two detectives nodded.

"Yeah I know the fellas. Hello, detectives."

"They're going to let me do the rundown and get the statement out of you."

"Aren't they kind?"

Hope and Finch sat down across from me. Fitzgerald leaned against the wall, thumbing through a manila folder. Hope threw a legal pad, a bunch of papers and some folders down on the table. He clicked in the top of his pen. Before he started to jot down some notes he looked up to address me.

"They caught an unidentified female D.O.A. on

Charles Street early in the morning."

"They didn't say it was Carlson?"

He flipped back a page on his legal pad and read through his brief notes on his previous phone conversation.

"...Ah No...He said she was still unidentified, presumed to be the leaser, Samantha Carlson. I.D. on the body's going to take a while. You've overloaded the morgue."

"No one can ID her?"

"Blunt trauma to the head. She was killed with a dumb bell. A weight. Her face was bashed in pretty severely. And the level of decomposition puts the time of death... Lawson probably killed her about a week ago. It sounded pretty ugly."

"I didn't see it...exactly."

"That's probably a good thing."

"...Yeah"

Finch threw a tap recorder on the table. Hope flipped back to a clean page on his pad.

"Give me all ya got."

Hours passed. I could barely keep my eyes open when everything had been said and done. Mary and Renee exited the precinct on either side of me. It was pitch black.

"Come on. I want to get away from this dump as fast as human possibly; before they charge me with something."

Renee was trying to keep her distance but was upset by my comment.

"What are they going to charge you with?"

"I don't know. Weapons charges, nothing too major I hope."

"You hope? What if--"

"Don't worry. The chief of D's was that fat guy in the lieutenant's office. He and I go way back. He'll definitely trying and indict me on something."

"Not funny. I hope you're wrong"

"That's not very likely, now is it?"

Mary finely broke her silence.

"Don't be an ass, Rupert."

"Thank you, Mary. So there, Mickey."

Mary looked over both of us before querying, "Mickey?"

Caught in yet another crossfire, I pushed on, ignoring the comment and hoping Mary would eventually do the same. Renee immediately recoiled and timidly spaced herself from the two of us.

"Okay. I should be going. Get some rest."

"Hey, wait. Where are you going?"

"Not sure. Some hotel"

"Which one?"

"Whichever. Bye, Mary."

"Not back to Roberto?"

"No. Bye, Graves."

"Wait."

I left Mary by the corner and followed Renee for a few paces.

"Your purse is in Staten Island."

"Ha-ha. You got me there. How 'bout a loan?"

I got out my wallet. I handed her my credit card.

"Try to not max it out before morning."

"Can't promise anything. I'll call Pierce about my purse. Thanks. Bye, again."

"Yeah"

Mary was tired and sullen. I wasn't in the mood to talk. I had talked enough. I waved down a cab.

"Are you going to fill me in?"

"No"

"You didn't really start sleeping with your secretary, did you? ..."

Mary got into the cab. I cracked my neck and followed. I was too tired to get bitched at or to bitch myself. I knew I was in the doghouse, which pissed me off because as I recalled she was the one that walked out. And she was the one who let herself back in. And I wasn't responsible for all the bullshit at the depot. Still, I felt guilty and nothing felt right. I hoped some rest would help, but I wasn't optimistic.

The front of the building was taped off. There was still a uniform in front of the building.

"Hey Sanders"

"Hey Graves. Mrs. Graves."

"We're good to go in, right?"

"Yeah. They said your good. Just bust the seal."

"Goodnight, Sanders."

We walked around to the alley. The back door was locked. I struggled for my keys. We made it to my landing. I looked back to the corner where Jensen had hidden days before. I looked back at the door. I pulled down the crime scene tape. I opened the door and broke the NYPD crime scene seal sticker placed across the door.

The apartment had been searched with less than a delicate touch; undoubtedly the tender touch of the brilliant forensic officers employed by the NYPD. There was yet another note under the door from Norman and Claudia. I put the note on the table. I didn't open it. I said that I would sleep in the guest room.

"You don't have to."

"It's fine. I like it in there."

"Goodnight, then."

I headed down the hall. Mary grabbed my swinging hand.

"I don't want to sleep alone."

She led me farther down the hall and into our room. We fell asleep lying next to each other, fully clothed and exhausted. I woke up fully clothed and alone.

The sun was piercing through the shades in the bedroom. The imprint from where Mary had slept was still there. The bandages on my head and torso were crusty with dried blood. My shirt was ripped and soiled.

Mary was cleaning up the room, putting the excess tape

and broken glass into a garbage bag. She didn't notice me until I was a foot away.

"Ah! Jesus, Rupert."

"Hey sorry"

"You scared the shit out of me."

"Yeah. I could tell."

"Somebody really went through the apartment."

"Yeah. Fucking forensics. You made any coffee?"

"It's like 2 o'clock. Here sit down. I'll make it. You smell terrible. It woke me up. Can you shower with the bandage on?"

I peeled off the bandage on my head. It still hurt.

"You should've gone to the hospital."

"I hate hospitals."

"Right. Where's the coffee?"

"In the cupboard"

"No. It's not."

I double-checked.

"I wasn't lying."

"We just bought some the other day."

"We?"

I was checking the cupboards in a futile attempt to avoid any awkwardness and any eye contact. I opened the fridge. The coffee was sitting on the top shelf.

"She put it in the fridge."

"How long have you been sleeping with her?"

"Why? Do you care?"

"I'm still your wife."

"By what fucked up barometer do you measure up to being a wife? You left. Or is that not how you remember it?"

"No, I haven't forgotten, Rupert. And if you want me to leave, I can do it again. But I kept calling and I came back. You know I never did that for anyone I've ever been with."

"This is all so fucking weird."

"Weird?"

"Yeah. Fucking weird. I got bodies dropping all around me. I'm dodging bullets, looking for lost fucks, dealing with cops, probably facing time or losing my business, saving secretaries and clients and estranged wives. Fucking weird shit, Mary. Okay?"

"Okay"

"Good. I hate this girly flavored coffee shit."

"So what do you want me to do?"

"I don't want to be in charge of you. Okay?"

"Okay"

"I just want to...be. I just want to be."

"...With me or with her?"

"For fuck's sake"

"How the fuck am I supposed to know, Rupert? I have to ask, don't I?"

"You left me. I didn't leave you."

I didn't know what to say for a few seconds. I just watched the coffee drop into the pot.

"I think we could give it another shot. We could go see somebody. If we really work at it, it could be like it used to be."

"No, it can't. When we were good, we were good. That was years ago, and I don't see that happening again. Not after years in duress."

"Why not?"

"Because shit happens and things change. I still love you, but it's different. Okay. Can we leave it at that?"

"Different could still be good?"

I hugged her as she stood there nearly sobbing. I didn't answer her.

"You had two fucking years to come to your senses. I get some time. Okay."

She smiled as I brushed off the tears.

"Don't smile or laugh, 'cause you don't get to write this shit off as me not taking it seriously. I'm just, you know, being sweet."

"Okay"

"Okay."

I walked out of the kitchen. Her perfume, her hair, her hands, everything was back just as it had been before. It was hard to handle. I wanted to jump her where she stood. She may have looked better than she ever did before. Two years changed her. I wasn't sure what the last two years had done to me. I wasn't sure what the last two days had done to me.

Back then I was confused. She was mine with three fucking words. You can guess which three. What were three words to me? I only mean a third of the shit I say. I had to mean one word of it. But I still hesitated. I had almost convinced myself when I found myself wandering towards the table by the door. I just wanted to look into the guest room so I could see Renee's things. Maybe I was looking for her too. But I wasn't sure. I wasn't even sure what I was looking for. Hence another dilemma. Should one ever abandon something good for the chance at something great? And which woman was which something?

Mary snapped me out of my wandering and wondering.

"Rupert."

I spun around.

"What? Yeah"

"I can't believe Norman and Claudia are still leaving notes."

"I've been avoiding them for days. I guess I owe them some face time."

"Now? Here, wait for a cup."

I waited a few seconds and she passed me a mug.

"Still just black, right?"

"Some things can't change."

I shut the apartment door behind me and knocked on Norman and Claudia's door. The coffee burnt my tongue. I was definitely ill suited for company in my bloody, putrid clothes. I was playing with the rip in my shirt from the bullet, enlarging it as I waited for Norman or Claudia to answer the door. But Norman and Claudia weren't suitable for company in their own respect. Norman finally answered the door with the paper in his hand.

"Oh, Mr. Graves."

"Hello, Norman. How are you?"

"Oh, well...as well as can be expected. I take it you saw... downstairs."

"Yes, quite the mess."

"Indeed. Tragic. Five people killed. And I thought this was a safe part of town. I can't imagine how they got in."

"You never know with these kinds of people."

"The police didn't even want Claudia and I to stay here. And they wouldn't let us go anywhere near the mess."

"It wasn't something you wanted to see."

"You saw it?"

"What did you want to talk to me about?"

"Oh, yes. Well, we left notes almost everyday."

"You could always knock or even call."

"We don't want to—uh--disturb you. Is that blood?"

"Dried blood"

"Are you all right?"

"Fine, it's barely a scratch."

"Oh, but that's a lot of blood. You're going to have to get rid of that shirt. I don't think that can be mended."

"I think you're right."

"You know, I used to be about your size. I may have some old shirts that would fit you. I'll get them out for you."

"That's generous, Norman, but I've got plenty of shirts. I just wanted to come over and see what you wanted--"

"Oh let me get Claudia."

He shut the door in my face, completely oblivious to my faces proximity to the doorway. I cracked my neck. Claudia reopened the door a matter of seconds later.

"Hello, Detective Graves."

"Hello, Claudia"

"Did you see that there was a gun fight downstairs?"

"It was hard to miss."

"Norman and I didn't hear a thing."

"I'm not surprised."

"Why's that?"

"Uh-- He used a silencer. It lessens the sound of the shots. They sound like--"

"I know what a silencer is, Detective Graves."

"Right. Claudia, it's just Mr. Graves. I'm not a--"

Claudia huffed and said, "Oh, fine. Well, if you're not a police officer, whom should we give this to?"

There it was. A few pieces of leather sewed together and folded into a five inch by four-inch rectangle. Just a fucking wallet.

I didn't realize whose it was at first or what it meant. I was holding the coffee mug to my mouth while I used my other hand to open the wallet. I cracked my neck. It was worn down, but was at one point a nice wallet. Paul Jensen's driver's license was visible through the clear plastic.

The wallet stirred up some lingering sentiments of guilt coupled with those of disgust and ineptitude. I hadn't solved the puzzle, found Michael Lawson, put together who killed who, gotten the whole story from Heather or done any of a hundred things that I could have and probably should have done. I didn't know who killed Hal, Ron, Mr. Gonetti or even Paul Jensen. I knew they were dead but I didn't know why they had to die. The murder of the girl in the bathtub in the village who I assumed was Samantha Carlson was still an open investigation. I expected Heather killed her in some fit of drug-induced rage or in an act of desperation. I didn't know much. But I knew me. And I knew that I would never really know the whole truth. People died, whatever the reason was, it wasn't a good reason. That's usually how it goes with these sorts of people, this sort of quicksand and me.

All I could do in that moment was stare at the wallet.

There was temporary solace in the assumption that all the murderers were murdered and the dust was settling. I wanted to push the mysteries of the quicksand into the dark recesses of my memory and focus on more familiar domestic troubles.

It was like old times. I had done what was necessary to escape alive, in one piece and a little richer. I had gone back to what I knew, where I felt safe and the people I trusted as I had done so often. I always figured change sucked. I didn't know if I was right. I never bothered to test the validity of my assumption. I had an image to maintain, a façade to protect. The world could change, but I could be content as a disassociated spectator.

I concentrated on the photo in his driver's license. I could see myself going back to the apartment and tucking away the wallet in a shoebox, taking it out in ten years and saying remember that poor bastard and that heap of shit you made your way through because you were so cool. I sighed and shook my head, contemplating why I had to be like I was. I resented what had become of me. I resented what I had done, and what so many others had done. Usually these moments of angst and resentment passed, fleeting moments in the night, but this time it was different. There was something about his driver's license: Jensen's eyes, his shaggy hair, his damn befuddled face, his unwitting naivety, his fucking innocence, his age. It all amassed into the tiny little spark that brought my matchstick house down in flames. I was focused on his birth date when I spoke again.

"He was twenty-fucking-seven."

"What?"

"He was twenty seven."

"I see. So you know him?"

"--Knew him. He died a few days ago."

"Terrible shame. Twenty-seven, you say?"

"Evidently"

"We found it a few days ago. It was wedged between

the grates over by the edge of the stairwell. Norman nearly threw out his back bending over to pick it up. We tried the number on the license but it was out of service. I trust you can return it to whoever should have it...even though you aren't a detective anymore."

"I'll take care of it."

"Was he consorting with the criminals responsible for downstairs?"

"If you mean me... then yes."

"Oh...Are you all right Mr. Graves?"

"Not ever. Sorry for not coming around sooner and thanks again."

"Oh wait--"

I waited. Claudia scampered off. Norman still had the paper in his hands. He looked down through the spectacles balancing at the end of his nose. He read over a headline.

"You know, there was another shooting yesterday too... in Brooklyn."

"Quicksand's contagious."

He looked up through his spectacles. Claudia reappeared. She reappeared with four perfectly starched white shirts.

"Norman never wears them. He used to be your size so they should fit. I don't think your going to be able to mend that shirt."

"Very kind of you. Thank you."

I used a free forefinger from my right hand in which I was holding my mug. I hung the four hangers over the finger. I still had the wallet open in my left hand. I managed to open my door, juggling things in both hands. Norman was still in the doorway of his apartment. His spectacles looked as if they could topple off his nose at any moment.

"Regret and guilt aren't always bad things, Mr. Graves. They can guide us to noble pursuits."

"What's a noble pursuit?"

"That's for you to figure out."

Norman grinned. He shut the door. Mary was going through the drawers in the kitchen.

"We should go to the store."

"Right"

"What did Norman and Claudia have to say?"

"Not much, the usual, some parting words of wisdom and some shirts."

"What a surprise."

"Do you regret leaving?"

"No. I regret it took so long for me to gather myself. But I need that time, after everything. Didn't you?"

I had sat down on the couch. I unbuttoned my ratty shirt. Mary continued speaking.

"When I was in Bordeaux, there was this family that lived next door. They brought their children to the beach everyday of the summer without fail, always a few hours before sunset."

I was examining the wallet and its contents more meticulously on the couch. He had a couple of credit cards, a few dollars, some other plastic cards and forms of ID. Buried at the bottom of the cash pocket was a photograph. It was folded in half, tattered and bent. There were some almost indiscernible words written on the back.

"These kids and their parents would carry chairs, umbrellas, everything out each day. The parents would sit under the umbrellas and the kids would make castles, do whatever."

It was a picture of Paul Jensen, two women and two children. Paul had his arm around one woman who had a young child sitting in her lap. I had never seen her before but I assumed she was Jensen's girlfriend.

"But the parents, the mother and the father sat fifteen feet away from each other. The mother painted under her umbrella and the father read a book under his."

The other woman was Heather Lawson. The child in her lap was older. I'm not sure how old. With my knowledge of children he could've been 2 or 12. But my best guess was that he was about 6. He was holding a birthday cake. The cake had 'Mike' spelled out on it. Heather was barely smiling, and blankly staring at the camera, not her son or the cake. Mike was smiling. I flipped over the photo, after spotting 'Mike' on the cake. I struggled but made out the words on the back. The note read, 'Michael- 7, Haley- 7 months'.

"They had their space. At the time it seemed a bit odd."

I startled Mary and interrupted the end of her story. I hadn't been paying attention anyways. And this was quite the bombshell. I tore off my shirt and grabbed a shirt Norman had given me. I ran into the bedroom. My father's gun was in a shoebox in the floor of my closet. I removed it, slammed in the clip and cocked it. I ran out of the bedroom and out of the apartment.

"This bitch's been playing me since the get-go."

I was down the stairs when I heard Mary yell after me.

"Wait. Rupert! Where are you going? Rupert!"

I didn't have time for her or for explanations. I didn't have much time for anything. I hailed a cab. I should've put it together. My stupidity had buoyed to the surface. All the rage I had been targeting inward transferred to a new external target, the real bitch. Everything inciting me to scorn myself mutated into fuel, and I needed to find Michael Lawson.

CHAPTER EIGHTEEN

I gave another 100-dollar bill to the cabbie. I was focused as I brushed past the doorman at Leo Lawson's Park Avenue spread.

"Hello. Sir. You can't--"

"I don't have time--"

"You're Mr. Lawson's friend."

I stopped before entering the elevator and turned back. I removed the photo from my pocket.

"No. I wasn't a friend."

"He was murdered last night."

"I know. Do you recognize her?"

"Um. Yeah. I recognize all of them."

"You do?"

"Sure."

"The kid that was staying with Mr. Lawson--"

"Mike. Yeah, that's him with the cake. He's a cute kid."

"I bet. How long has been staying here?"

"Two weeks or so"

"Is he still upstairs?"

"I believe so. Rosanna upstairs, she's been speaking to the police. The police and Mr. Lawson's lawyer were here until just a little while ago."

"I'm going to go up there, straighten some things out. If you see-- the girl..."

"Yeah?"

"Don't do anything. Act normal. Let her up. As soon as you do, call the police. Tell them that there's a woman who is armed and dangerous trying to kidnap a kid."

"Dangerous?"

"And armed. Make the call if she shows up."

I walked to the elevator.

"What makes you think she'll show up?"

I didn't answer. I hit the button for the top floor. Rosanna answered the door.

"You! Why are you here?"

"Whose boy is that?"

"What boy?"

"Yeah Okay."

I walked by her.

"You can't see him."

"Not yet."

"No. No. Mr. Lawson didn't want anyone to know he was here."

"Yeah that was a good plan up until about dusk yesterday when he was killed. He's dead and you can't protect him from his mommy."

"Yes but Mr. Leo's son is on his way. He is going to take care of the boy."

"Because he's the boy's father, right?"

"...Yes"

"Okay. Well until then I think you two should go somewhere... less obvious."

"Why?"

"Because the dust's settling and the little boy's mother is bound to try to get him back, and she's very crazy and very scary and very dangerous."

Rosanna could see how serious I was.

"Where will we go?"

"I'll think about it. Will you get the boy?"

"Right now?"

"Yeah. We need to go right now."

"All right. I'll get him."

Rosanna walked down the hall into a room where the boy was watching television. There was a portable phone by the couch in the living room. I took out my wallet. I pulled out Hope's business card. It was his official business card with the cute little NYPD logo and his title and everything. I dialed his number. An operator picked up.

"15th Precinct."

"Detective Hope"

"Hold on."

Rosanna and Mike were ready and waiting in the hall by the elevator I walked up. I was still on hold. The kid had a little backpack on. He was holding a toy car.

"Who is he?"

The kid looked tragically unaware. He had his mother's eyes.

"My name's Graves."

"My name's Mike."

I was still on hold. Rosanna opened the door. I wasn't paying attention. As Hope picked up, Rosanna yelped, "Ah! Dios mio!"

My head swung. 'Detective Hope' rang into my right ear. My eyes fixed upon the female figure just outside the doorway. She held a Glock 22 C in one hand.

"Hang up the phone."

I abided. My father's gun was stuffed in the back of my pants but I had the sneaking suspicion I didn't want to play quick draw with a deranged woman who had already had me beat. The boy ran up to the woman.

"Mommy, why do you have a gun?"

"For protection, baby. Come here. Did you miss me? Yeah, you did. I've been to get to you. Trying so hard."

She bent down to hug the kid, but her eyes didn't flinch.

"I was with grandpa. He's really cool and his apartment is really big. I want to show you my room."

"I know. Maybe later. I've been so worried. But I found you. And you even kept your back pack safe."

"Aunt Heather said I had to."

"And you did. Will you do something for me now? Take your cars and go into that room over there and make a racetrack. Go ahead."

"Mom...come on."

"Please... Here, leave your back pack"

"Okay. Oh Mom, that's Rosanna. And that's... Graves."

"I know who they are, honey. So go ahead"

The kid scuttled into the other room. I watched as his mother gestured for him to close the door. She pushed Rosanna back towards me. She rifled through the backpack. As she struggled, I could see that bundles of cash were taped to the lining. It looked like more than half a million, but that's always how it is. In actuality, less than four hundred grand made it to safekeeping in the backpack.

"Nice job, Samantha."

"Move back over there. Keep your hands up. Do you have a gun?"

"I had one. But it looks to be in your hands right now?"

"Shut up. Turn around. Turn!"

I turned quickly.

"There ya go"

"Yeah. You! You, take the gun out of the back of his pants and kick it over here."

Rosanna quivered as she did what she was told. The old forty-five glided down the hardwood floors.

"So smart. So smart. You can't do anything right! Where is he? Where's the old man?"

"He's dead."

"Shut up. Where?"

"He got shot three times yesterday by his driver, trying to save a daughter that was long dead."

"I don't believe you."

Rosanna spoke for the first time.

"It's true, Sam. Mr. Leo's dead."

I lowered my arms.

"That's right. He's dead. You've got your son. You're ex is on his way from Japan or where-the-fuck-ever. You must have your money. So why don't you just leave."

"You aren't in charge. You don't get to decide anything."

"Whatever you say"

"You had to get so fucking involved. And that smug bastard, he wouldn't give us any help for seven years. When I first asked for help, he laughed. Then, he started sending her or a doorman to tell me I wasn't welcome. He wouldn't welcome his own grandson. We could barely get by. And he didn't care, he and his fucking witch of a wife. I hope they enjoy burning in hell together. Move over there! By the couches!"

Rosanna ran over and sat down on one couch. She was trying to mute her hysterics and tears. I took my time and moved towards the other couch.

"I have to congratulate you. Usually, I can tell when I'm getting fed shit from the get-go, but with you-- I really just thought that junk had turned your brain to shit. I didn't think were capable of this."

"Shut the fuck up."

"Do you shoot up and smoke in front of the kid? Does he get what it is yet? Because--"

Samantha ran up and shut the door the study. Then she ran down towards me.

"Shut the fuck up. You have no fucking idea what I've been through for him. So you shut up. You don't get to talk."

"For him? I don't know about that. You seem pretty hell-bent on self-preservation--"

"Now, I want to know exactly where Michael is?"

"Mike Sr., you mean?"

"Yes."

"Couldn't tell you... exactly."

"Do you really want to play dumb?"

"No. But you know, I feel dumb. I can't believe I didn't realize it was you who broke in to the office. I mean, you had been waiting in my office alone, so you must have looked around, right? You found the gun, decided you needed it. But you couldn't take it right away because I'd notice and Renee was there. So you decided to break in later. You knew the shit had hit the fan and you managed to bring me into the line of fire. Yeah. I should've seen it all coming."

"Yeah some detective you are. You couldn't find Michael."

"I'm glad I didn't. Poor guy. I'd choose an anonymous existence in Japan over you too."

"Me! Me! Look at him. He left. He went to fucking Japan, so that he could get away. I was pregnant and he didn't want the fucking responsibility. ...That's what he told me: that he didn't want the responsibility of a son. And he left me alone with nothing. He made his son a bastard. Mike has had to grow up poor and with out a father because of that spoiled coward."

"So you want him dead."

"No, I want his life."

"Jesus. Like you wanted Jensen's life?"

"I didn't want that to happen. He was—I didn't want that to happen."

"Like you didn't want to kill three innocent men instead of me."

"That was your fault."

"My fault? I don't think so. And how about Heather? She was there for you and you beat her skull in with a fucking dumb bell. Whose fault was that? Huh? Thank God the kid didn't watch you do that."

Samantha was in tears and brought the gun up to eye level, pointing it at my head.

"You shut up!"

"Yeah, you keep saying that. But listen to what you've done. Look at what you're doing... Your son is in the next room for Christ's sake. Do you think he isn't going to hear the shots or see the bodies? What's he going to think?"

"Everything I've done is for my son. He's going to have a good life. He deserves that. He's owed that."

"Sure. He is. You're right. He's gotten the shaft so far, especially with you being fucking crazy and all."

"I don't want to hear you talk."

"That's why she brought him here, right? Heather. After her mom died and your terrible plan blew up, she knew you guys weren't safe."

"My plan?"

"Did she want to run? Was that it? You wanted a normal life, right? You wanted to stand and fight. You didn't want to be running from drug lords. You wanted a white picket fence and Mike to get a dad who liked to play wiffle-ball with him. Am I on target? How's my detecting, Samantha?"

"You don't know anything."

"I know Heather must have taken him. You went somewhere and when you came back Mike was gone. She knew everything was going to shit and she didn't want Mikey, there, in the middle. Did you not see she was helping him?"

"By taking my son?"

"I'd say by saving your son. I mean look at how this shit turned out. You were scared to do anything. You looked for easy money and an easy way out. You found Rolando. You fucked everything up, and started killing people as if it were a fucking remedy."

"You don't know anything."

She was high on something and she wanted to break down. But she had some real resolve in her.

"Yeah, I do. I know what you're going to do now."

"So what am I going to do now?"

"You're going to take your son and run. That's all you can do. You've got to stop killing your way out of trouble, because it doesn't work."

"It has so far."

"It hasn't worked. The more people you kill the deeper you sink. You know it. You know you're in too deep. You are a better psychopath than most. Most don't make it this long with out being mowed down or getting strapped with a set of bracelets, but do you really think you can get away? You can't. I'm sorry. You can't."

She prepared to shoot me.

"I'm right. And do you know what happens to Mike? ...Do you?"

"He'll be fine."

"Oh shit no. You're going to get caught. Even with a backpack full of money, you won't make it to wherever you think you can go. It's a long, strange trip to where you need to go. You fucked up your domestic freedoms."

"We'll make it, together."

"You won't make it, period."

"Yes, we will."

"And when you're dead or in jail, he'll be alone."

"No"

"Not only will his father have abandoned him, but his mother too."

"I will never...never abandon him!"

"You already have. You have fucking committed him to a lifetime of pain and suffering. Have you seen foster homes here? You know how child services works? Ten to a room, no supervision, no help, no fun, and no one adopts six year olds, no matter how good their pedigree is. And he doesn't have a fat trust fund. He'll be fucked. That's just how it is. He'll be just like you."

"No. He won't. That won't happen."

"He'll be fucked. He'll end up state raised,

institutionalized and then probably imprisoned by the state that raised him."

"You don't know that."

"I've seen it happen. He'll be royally fucked. Worse if you kill me, if you kill her or anyone else. That's just one more person he'll know his mother killed."

She was sobbing, broken. I took the opportunity and pounced.

"Do you think he'll love you when he finds out what you've done? I don't. Who could love you?"

She blinked and a round went off, but I got the gun. I sighed. I threw her to the ground. She sobbed uncontrollably. Rosanna screamed and ran off to get the phone. She started dialing 911. But I was hoping they were already on their way. Rosanna was going through the motions and telling the operator everything. I was breathing.

"Fuck. Stupid psychotic bitch. Christ almighty, woman. Am I lucky or cursed? You are so fucking nuts. I mean they have got to send you right to the motherfucking puzzle factory. Shit. That's like the twelfth fucking heart attack you've almost given me."

I collapsed down on to a chair, cracking my neck furiously. Mike appeared at the doorway to the office with his hands over his ears.

"Mommy"

Samantha sprung to her feet, still weeping. I stopped her before she could make it to him. I threw her down and scooped up the kid.

"Michael"

"Heath--I mean...Samantha, stay back. I'm warning you stay back."

"Mommy..."

The kid was getting upset but I didn't want anything else happening. The kid didn't deserve it. And my heart couldn't handle any more action. The kid began to fuss and cry. He still had his hands over his ears because of the gunshot.

I handed him to Rosanna. They scrambled back into the study. I wasn't paying attention to Samantha as I struggled to close the door to the study. There was silence. Samantha had stopped weeping. She sat still on the hardwood floors by the hall. I wasn't fully paying attention when she first spoke. I was peeking into the study to see Rosanna holding the child.

"He isn't looking, is he?"

"What?"

"Don't let him see."

I didn't have my gun aimed at her. It was resting at my side. I didn't see anything. I heard the shot.

Her blood and pieces of her skull coated the hall. My father's forty-five had fallen out of her limp hand. The blood pooled on the hardwood floor, dripping down into the living room. I stood, statuesque, with my gun at my side, jaw slightly drooped and Samantha Carlson's bloodied body a few feet away.

The cops emerged from the stairway a few seconds later. An eternity too late.

CHAPTER NINETEEN

The sun set and the moon was making an appearance when I finally got through with my final round of interrogations. Hope didn't question it all too much. It made sense given that Heather Lawson had been identified as the battered corpse in Carlson's apartment, and given that the three hundred and ninety four thousand dollars found in Mike Jr.'s back pack matched up with a suspicious withdraw August Summers had made from an account a month earlier. Hope said I was 'ballsy, but brainless'. It was a shock to the system. It felt good to hear, but I felt like shit. So Hope released me with the assurance he wouldn't recommend indicting me and that my official complaint about police response time to Park Ave apartments and container depots in Brooklyn would most definitely not be taken seriously. I was physically exhausted, but mentally revitalized, when I got back to the apartment.

The door was locked as I tried to get back in. I didn't have my keys. Mary answered the door.

"You're all right, I take it?"

I was leaning up against the wall.

"What are you doing? Come in."

I hesitated to slink inside, but did.

"You got something on your new shirt."

"Dried blood again."

"Yours?"

"Nope"

"Tell me what happened."

"I don't want to."

On the table were a note, my wad of nearly ten thousand dollars and my credit card. I picked the note up from underneath the credit card. It was from Renee.

"Yeah. Renee stopped by for a few painful minutes. She got her things, dropped off your card and all this cash. I would've gone to the Plaza if I was--"

"I'm not staying."

"What?"

"I can't love you like I did. You and I both need something new and clean. Not worn out. You were right to leave. I'm sorry to have put you through all this shit. It just takes me a long time to figure these things out."

"Rupert..."

"The apartment's yours. There are some papers you should look over in the desk. And I'll talk to you soon, but I need to go now."

I picked up my keys, half the cash and Renee's note. I took off the two keys for the apartment. I put them on the table. I walked out the door backwards with the piece of hotel stationary.

"Rupert, I don't know what to say."

"Well, don't say 'goodbye'. Just say 'It was nice seeing you'."

I'd seen her cry maybe three times in all the time we'd been together. I thought she may cry then, but she didn't. She laughed ever so slightly at what I said. Then Mary gave a small nod from the doorway, looked at me and said, "You are an asshole, Rupert."

"That I am."

I grinned and gave her a wave. I walked off, not away,

just off. I didn't run or leave in the cover of the night. I did a shitty thing as best I could, knowing it was definitely best for me and possibly best for Mary too.

I've found that when I walk with a purpose, the world is at a standstill. The people I pass are part of the scenery. I'm independent of them. I love walking with purpose. There's an elegant clarity that comes with purpose; a satisfying enlightenment.

I walked into the hotel, through the hotel lobby and into the elevator with purpose. I walked out of the elevator, down the hall and up to room 313 with purpose. The purpose answered the door in sweat pants and a t-shirt.

"Hey"

"Hey yourself"

"I stopped by earlier and talked--Holy shit are you bleeding again?"

"Not really"

"Does that mean you're okay?"

"No"

"Okay. Let me be clear. Are there armed men outside or are you currently in danger--"

"Ha-ha. No"

"Good. I know you hate people guessing things. So do you want to tell me what's happened now?"

"Ya know...I would honestly love to."

I was serious, but she didn't believe it.

"Deadpan sarcasm. Something new. I'll have to remember to stop caring when you show up with--"

I made a half step and kissed her. I pinned her against the door. She was a bit reluctant to accept my advance but did.

"Graves..."

"What?"

"Your wife"

"No wife."

"She said you were going to try to make it work."

"We're not. But you and I are."

"Is that right?"

"It sure is."

"So that's why you're here?"

"Yeah"

"You've fallen for me?"

"Yeah"

"And you think that's okay with me?"

"Yeah"

"...Yeah?"

"Yup."

"I'm not finished with my questions."

We rolled off the door and into the room, embracing, kissing, doing all that mushy shit. She didn't get to finish her questions. It felt right and clean. It felt like the end of a lot of long days and the beginning of a lot of good ones.

My foot had been wedged between the hotel room door and the carpet to keep it open. I rolled away into the room, taking my foot with me. The door shut slowly. I stopped for a second to say, "I want to tell you something."

"What?"

"You're fired."

She smiled. The door slammed shut, but it didn't stay that way.

Roberto Carpagni arrived at our door seconds after it shut. I couldn't see him of course. We were already in the room and on the bed. He was disheveled, wearing a sweat suit, and carrying a cute little three-fifty-seven. He was kind enough to knock, but that was the limit of his kindness and the beginning of another story that you probably wouldn't want to hear much about.

THE END

221

ABOUT THE AUTHOR

R.T. Graves lives in Connecticut. He is a fraud investigator and consultant. He completed *Uptown Quicksand*, his first book, in 2008. Due to the publicity of crimes recounted, Graves waited seven years to publish.